DOUBLE DRAMA AT STARLIGHT ACADEMY

RAGGED BEARS
Published by Ragged Bears Ltd.
The Granary
Compton Pauncefoot
Somerset BA22 7EL, UK

First published 2013

1 3 5 7 9 10 8 6 4 2

A CIP catalogue record for this book is available from the British Library

ISBN 978-1-85714-422-2

Printed in Poland

www.ragged-bears.co.uk

DOUBLE DRAMA AT STARLIGHT ACADEMY

Jess Renison

For Katie

with love

Jess Renison

Ragged Bears

Contents

Chapter 1: *The Synthetic Twins*   *3*

Chapter 2: *Back in the Woods*   *20*

Chapter 3: *Wilderness Club*   *32*

Chapter 4: *Poems on Trees*   *40*

Chapter 5: *Quiz Night*   *53*

Chapter 6: *The Arrival of Miss Spitzer*   *64*

Chapter 7: *It all goes wrong*   *75*

Chapter 8: *The Woodshed Theatre*   *85*

Chapter 9: *More Trouble*   *104*

Chapter 10: *Founder's Day*   *116*

Chapter 11: *Camping Out*   *128*

Chapter 12: *Double Drama*   *141*

Chapter 1: *The Synthetic Twins*

When the first few days of the Spring Term were cancelled because of heavy snow, Cassie was so annoyed that she kicked over the snowman in the garden.

'Hey – mind you don't break a leg,' called her dad from the kitchen window where he was washing up after breakfast. 'I'm not paying for all those ballet lessons to see your career ruined by a snowman. Anyway,' he laughed, 'I seem to remember that this time last term you were busy working out how to escape from that place.'

'Yeah, well that was when I thought everyone would be all strict and boring,' said Cassie, frowning and rubbing her foot because the snowman had been harder than she thought. 'Oh, it's not fair!' she wailed, stamping in the snow like a three-year-old. 'What if it never stops snowing and school just closes forever and I never get to see anyone ever again?'

'A bit unlikely I think,' said her dad, chuckling in an infuriating way as he closed the window.

It was true: she *had* thought everyone at Starlight Academy was too obsessed with rules at first, but by the end of term, she had got used to all of that, and it wasn't so bad. Plus, she got to share a bedroom with all of her best friends – almost like sharing a flat together – and there was always so much going on. Even though she knew school was closed, Cassie still felt as if she was missing out on all the fun. She kept imagining the term going on without her, the gossip and the laughs just out of earshot, the big production getting underway behind her back. Cassie had already had her moment of complete happiness when she starred as Clara in *The Nutcracker* at the end of the previous term, and that was enough to keep her going until the next big dance production the following year. But now it was the turn of the actors: there would be a major drama production this term, and then the singers would get their time onstage with the summer musical production.

Clapping her gloved hands together for warmth, Cassie looked along the row of tall, red-brick houses that were squashed into line with her house, getting smaller and smaller as they disappeared down the street. Thin curls of smoke rose out of chimneys, and the smell of toast spilt out of open windows along with the morning shouts of family life. It gave her a warm, comfortable feeling: the feeling of home. The backs of the houses were a higgledy-piggledy mish-mash of porches and conservatories, balconies, decks and steps, some sparkling glass and steel, some crumbling wood and peeling paint, all tacked on without any thought for pattern or symmetry. And yet from the front, the houses all looked pretty much identical, except perhaps for their door colour. It reminded her with a pang of her friends at Starlight, all identical in their matching uniform, all performers of some kind – either dancers, singers or actors – but all with completely different characters.

'Hey!'

A snowball caught her on the back of the neck and she spun around to see Milo's head ducking behind the fence of the garden next door.

'There's no point hiding,' she called, 'I can see that little fluffy bobble on top of your hat.'

He laughed and popped up again.

'Isn't it great,' he said, 'second day off school already and the term hasn't even started yet.'

'Yeah, I suppose so,' Cassie replied, surreptitiously reaching behind her back for a scoop of snow from the toppled snowman and packing it into a hard ball. 'It's just that I so badly want to see my Starlight friends.'

Milo nodded thoughtfully and narrowed his eyes.

'So, your old friends aren't good enough for you any more?'

'They're good enough to throw snowballs at,' she replied, scoring a perfect shot in Milo's face.

He coughed and spluttered and shook himself like a dog coming out of the sea.

'Well anyway, if I'm still "starry" enough for you to hang out with, I was wondering if you wanted to go sledging. I got a new snow-board for Christmas. We could go to the Heath.'

'OK,' Cassie shrugged, 'nothing better to do.'

*   *   *

By the time the snow melted and school re-opened,
Cassie was so itchy to be gone, she felt as if she had
fleas. And then her dad seemed to take ages packing the
car – he kept unpacking and repacking everything in a
maddening way to get the best fit.

'Come *on*!' Cassie pleaded. 'If we don't get there in
time, someone might get my place in Fonteyn.'

'I don't think it quite works like that,' laughed her dad,
examining the luggage in the boot thoughtfully.

'But what if they do, and I get stuck in a dorm with
no one I know?' Cassie was beginning to feel genuinely
nervous at the thought.

'I'm pretty sure you stay in the same dorm for the
whole year, sweetheart,' he said absentmindedly, taking
her guitar out of the corner it had been wedged into and
wondering where else it might go. The car was crammed
full because Mr March was going straight on to the airport
after he had dropped Cassie off. He was usually a furni-
ture maker but recently he had started building designer
tree-houses for the rich and famous. He had a rock-star
client in California who wanted a tree-house bathroom
so that he could have a shower up amongst the leaves,
and he was making his first visit to the site to create his
design.

As they drove through the greying slush up the driveway
to school, they talked about his latest project.

'As soon as you get back,' said Cassie, 'I want you to
start making me a recording studio tree-house in our back

garden. For when I start my own band and everything.'

Her dad raised his eyebrows sceptically, 'Crazy, what these people spend their money on. There are millions of children in the world without water and he wants to have a shower up in a tree so that it feels like showering in the rain.'

'I've got an idea! Why don't you insist that he donates the same amount as whatever the tree-house costs to a water charity or something,' suggested Cassie.

'Actually that's not a bad idea,' said Mr March, nodding his head.

As their car crossed the drawbridge and the imposing front of Starlight Academy came into view – with its sandstone turrets and fairytale windows – Cassie felt nervous all over again, as if it was her first day once more. She had met up with Flo over the holidays, but it seemed ages since she had seen Jasmine and the two Year 8 girls Bella and Megan who shared their dorm. She wondered if they would still like her, would still remember her even. And would they be the same themselves? Or would they have changed over the holidays and have met other people and no longer be interested in having a Year 7 girl for a friend? In her desperation to find out, she clicked her belt and opened the door before the car had quite stopped. Her dad reined her back in.

'Hang on! Hang on!' he laughed. 'Aren't you even going to say goodbye? I might as well have just flown over and parachuted you in.'

There were girls running about everywhere, weaving in and out of each other, bumping into each other, and tripping over the piles of bags heaped around the forecourt. It looked to Cassie for a moment like a colourful ant colony, except that they all squealed a lot more than ants, and jumped up and down, and hugged each other, which ants don't usually do.

'Cassie! You're here at last! We thought you must have got stuck up a tree somewhere.'

Bella came running over to her and gave her a hug, which from Bella was a fairly painful experience. Her round, rosy face was bubbling over with excitement.

'Look, Megan's parents are here.' She pointed to where an uber-stylish mum and hyper-cool dad stood by an opened-topped, old-fashioned sports car. 'And her mum said I could have her old Prada sunglasses, plus I'm going to a music festival with them at half term – I mean proper music, not my parents' sort of stuff – you know, camping with real rock-stars and everything.'

By now, Bella was flapping her hands and gasping with excitement.

'Can I get you a seat? Or a glass of water or something?' asked Cassie's dad, with a bemused smile.

'No, I'll be fine thanks,' said Bella, clapping her hands to her chest. 'Sorry, I'll calm down in a moment. Anyway, that's not until half term and there's plenty to look forward to before then.'

'Where are *your* folks anyway?' asked Cassie's dad, 'I wanted to return a book they lent me.'

'Oh, sorry,' grimaced Bella, 'was it some big fat thing

about churches in Eastern Europe? Or a yawnsome history of the Bible or something?'

'Not quite,' laughed Cassie's dad.

'They're over there talking to Mrs Frost.'

Bella pointed to where a woman who looked like Little Bo Peep stood talking to the headmistress in a long flowery dress, a straw bonnet tied under her chin with a flowing scarf. Bella's dad was standing alongside nodding eagerly, his few wisps of hair blowing in the wind. He wore huge red glasses and rainbow braces over a thick bobbly fisherman's jumper.

'I bet they're asking her if they can do an assembly on their collection of ancient woodwind instruments,' Bella groaned. 'I've begged and begged them not to, but I bet they will anyway. They were convinced we would be interested in doing a workshop on medieval tapestry but I managed to talk them out of it.'

'Workshop on medieval tapestry?' Megan had overheard the last part as she came towards them, 'I'd love that!'

'Hmm, I know you would,' said Bella, frowning disapprovingly. 'It's lucky we're such good friends or I wouldn't like you at all. Except for your cool parents of course – they're your saving grace.'

Bella and Megan had known each other since long before Starlight Academy: one a loud-mouthed, clownish actress and the other a quiet, studious musician, they had fought over a scooter on the first day of primary school and been firm friends ever since.

'Come on you guys!' Bella grabbed Cassie's and

Megan's arms. 'Let's go up to the dorm. I bet Jasmine's already up there making it all homely for us.'

Up in the dorm, Cassie's heart skipped a beat, just as it had the first time, when she caught a glimpse of the sea sparkling in the distance through their bedroom window. During the Autumn term there had been too much going on to get down to the sea, and she was determined that this term she would make it, one way or another. If she could do it legally, fine. If not … well, she wasn't a total goody-goody yet. As Bella predicted, Jasmine had already made the room cosy. Cassie gave her a big hug and Jasmine showed her the latest photos of her baby brother, who she was crazy about. Then she began to unpack her things. As she hung up her grey and red uniform, which had been badly ironed by her dad, she remembered how she had hated having to wear it at first. Now, looking at it gave her a warm feeling because it reminded her of all the good times she had had with her friends. Apart from her uniform and her dance outfits, there were her mother's ballet shoes, which she stored under her bed, a few pairs of jeans and jumpers, and the new neon-pink platform trainers she had got for Christmas. Finally, she put up the framed photo of her and Flo dancing, which Flo's brother Tom had taken at their New Year's Party.

Bella was still rattling away in the background. Megan was busy unpacking – and anyway had already heard most of Bella's holiday stories – so Bella was sitting on Jasmine's bed, treating her to some of the highlights:

'On New Year's Eve we drove for two hours to a freezing cold church for a concert of ancient music on ancient violins that lasted for three hours! Three hours! Well, all I can say is Starlight Academy is extremely fortunate that its leading actress is still alive to grace its hallowed stage – I'm telling you, I very nearly died of boredom.'

She turned to Megan, who was busy organising her books on the shelf above her bed.

'I bet *you* were at some celebrity party on New Year's Eve. Or your parents probably had Johnny Depp round or something.'

'Who?' said Megan absentmindedly. 'Oh, yes, we were at someone or other's house. Someone famous-ish I think. Can't remember who.' She was lying on her back reading a book by now. 'Mum took me to a bookshop yesterday and let me choose anything I wanted. It was so cool.'

'She told me you went to the new Jimmy Choo store in Chelsea,' Bella challenged.

'Did we? I don't know. We went to so many shops, I can't remember. But it was OK because I just sat in the changing rooms and read.'

'Actually, that's not OK, Megan! It's a crime. Designer labels are totally wasted on you – you might as well just wear my dad's Oxfam collection.'

She waltzed over to Megan's bed and whisked the book out of her hands.

'And stop reading! We've got important plans to make.'

Megan snatched her book back just as quickly, whacked Bella over the head with it and fell back on her bed.

'*You* have maybe. *I've* just got to a really good bit in *Pride and Prejudice.*'

'Yawn!' cried Bella, falling back onto her own bed in a deep coma. But she couldn't stay there for long: a few seconds later, she was back on her feet.

'Anyway, like I was saying, I've got some great ideas for tricks to play on teachers. It's the only thing that's kept me going all holidays.'

'How do you think them all up?' asked Jasmine, full of admiration.

'Actually, it's mostly whilst we're traipsing around art galleries. I always go straight for the pictures with loads of people in them, doing all sorts of ridiculous things and they give me ideas for tricks and stuff, which I dutifully jot down. I'm telling you, it's the only way to survive art galleries. God, if I never set foot inside another one as long as I live, I will die happy.'

The evening sun was slanting in through the window, painting the girls' faces pink.

'So, did you have a *completely* miserable holiday then?' Jasmine asked Bella with a look of deep concern.

'No, not really,' breezed Bella cheerily, 'we went to see loads of plays as well, so it was fine.'

'Talking of which,' Megan interrupted, peering over the top of her book, 'have you heard what play you're doing this term?'

'Well, the Years 7 and 8 one is always Shakespeare, and I've heard whisperings that it's going to be *As You Like It*, in which case I'm definitely going for the part of Rosalind.'

'I wonder if Abigail will go for Rosalind too,' said Jasmine wistfully. 'Oh, I hope I don't get torn between two friends. I won't know who to support.'

Everyone looked puzzled. Then Cassie asked, 'What are you talking about? Who's Abigail?'

'Abigail Rowan – in our year,' replied Jasmine, as if they were all a bit dim. 'You know, the one with that really cool sideways fringe. We met up in the holidays. It turns out she lives in the same village as my gran. She's an actress too you see, and I know she'll want to go for the main part because she's *so* good, she really is. We saw her as Annie at the local theatre in the holidays.'

'But not nearly as good as your friend Bella,' said Bella, pinching Jasmine's cheek, 'so she can pretty much forget it.'

'Oh no! I knew it would be like this,' cried Jasmine anxiously, 'I feel torn already.'

Bella laughed, 'Chill out Jasmine, I'm only joking.'

A bell rang and they all dropped what they were doing and rushed for the door.

'Yippee! It's always hot chocolate and muffins on the first night back,' whooped Bella as they fought each other to get out of the room and tumbled laughing down to supper.

The dining hall was raucous with the clank of dishes and

waves of excitable chatter. Every so often, Mrs Frost would chink on her glass with a spoon and the noise would die down for a bit, but then one burst of laughter would start it all off again, and after a while she stopped chinking and gave up with a shrug and a smile. As soon as they had entered the dining hall, Jasmine had broken away from them and gone to sit with her new friend, but once the last cups of hot chocolate were empty and every last crumb of toasted muffin had gone, she dragged Abigail and another girl over to where the others were sitting. Cassie knew Abigail from class last term, but they had never spoken much – that was until Abigail had made herself the spokesperson for the entire class when they had all turned against Cassie in the case of the poison pen.

'I brought Abigail over to say Hi,' said Jasmine proudly. 'And Lauren too, 'cos they're best friends.'

Abigail and Lauren were always together. Wherever Abigail went, Lauren went too. They were glued so tightly, it was a miracle Jasmine had managed to squeeze in between them.

'And *you*,' said Abigail, smiling sweetly at Jasmine and throwing her arm around her. '*You're* our best friend now too.'

'Hey, now we're triplets!' squealed Lauren, clapping her hands with delight.

It was true, Abigail and Lauren did look like twins, but mainly because Lauren had copied Abigail's haircut and they made a point of wearing the same clothes.

'*We're synthetic twins,*' they were always saying (and

14

Lauren would always explain straight away) – *'you know, like, not natural twins cause we weren't born twins, but synthetic, like synthetic food colourings, 'cause we made ourselves twins artificially.'* As they said the *'synthetic twins'* thing quite often, lots of people had heard this explanation a few times over and sometimes succeeded in stopping her at the beginning by saying it for her: *'We know, not like natural twins, etcetera'*.

'You'll have to get your hair cut like ours Jasmine,' said Lauren, fiddling with Jasmine's hair and making a false fringe for her, 'I think this style would look fab on you.'

Jasmine beamed with pleasure and looked around at the others as if to say *'Aren't they the best!'*

Abigail jumped up on the table (Mrs Frost had left the room) and sat swinging her legs.

'Cool Converse,' said Bella, instantly noticing Abigail's gold trainers.

'Thanks. What dorms are you lot in? We're in Piaf,' she continued, without waiting for an answer. 'You guys should come over – we're going to have a film night on Friday.' She whispered behind her hand, 'I've got a special behind-the-scenes DVD of *Wild Thing*.'

'Wow! How did you get that?' gasped Bella.

'My dad's in the film business,' said Abigail.

'What's *Wild Thing*?' asked Megan and they all groaned.

'It's only *the* film of the season,' said Bella, punching Megan's arm. 'It's got Jed Brogan in it. He's a college student who gets accused of a crime he didn't commit

15

and runs away from the police, and basically crosses the whole of America on a motorbike, getting into all sorts of other trouble.'

'But isn't it a Fifteen?' asked Jasmine nervously.

'Well, we all *look* about fifteen,' said Abigail. 'Anyway, we're going to watch it on my laptop in the dorm and I promise we won't be checking your ages on the door.'

Just then, Jasmine spotted Tara across the room and called out to her. When Tara eventually sauntered over, Jasmine gave her a spontaneous hug and she couldn't help looking pleased. In fact, they all felt pleased to see Tara, in spite of everything that had happened last term. It wasn't just that Mrs Frost had forbidden them ever to talk about the incident again, it did just seem so long ago. Even for Cassie, whom Tara had most hurt, it felt like a different lifetime, and she was genuinely pleased to see Tara back. Tara had a skiing tan, with white sunglasses marks, and she flicked her white-blonde hair over her shoulder as she swung herself up onto the table beside Bella and Abigail.

'Hey, you've been skiing too!' said Lauren. 'Me and Abigail went to Meribel.'

'Oh, I don't find the runs there challenging enough,' said Tara.

'No, me neither,' said Lauren, 'but we were snow-boarding this year and that makes a difference.'

'Yes, I did boarding last year, but I'm kind of over it now,' said Tara in a bored voice. 'I did a sponsored climb up Mont Blanc this year.'

Bella chinked a glass, Mrs Frost-style: 'Ahem! Excuse me, but when you lot have quite finished going on about how fantastic you are, maybe we could get back to this film night. So, Abigail, what does your dad do in the film business?'

'He's a director. He was one of the directors on *Wild Thing*, but you know, there were loads of them so it's not like he's super famous or anything.'

'Great,' moaned Bella. 'I'm like the only person in school whose parents aren't cool. It's not fair. Cassie's dad is in California making designer tree-houses for rock stars, Megan's dad is a record-producer, yours makes films, and mine is probably at home making brown bread and yoghurt.'

'When is this film night anyway?' asked Tara.

'Next Friday,' Lauren replied, 'in our dorm. But it's invites only.'

'Can't be next Friday,' said Tara, waggling her finger. 'I've organized a fund-raising quiz night in aid of a children's hospital.'

Everyone felt slightly annoyed with the way Tara had barged in and trampled all over their plans, but given that there was a children's hospital involved, it seemed somehow mean-spirited to say so.

'OK, I suppose we could do it on Saturday night instead,' said Abigail reluctantly.

'How come anyway?' asked Bella, giving Tara a suspicious look.

'You mean how come someone like me would do something like that?' smiled Tara.

'Well, that is kind of what I meant, yes.'

'It's the children's hospital that my baby sister was in before she died. I've been raising money for them for years.'

Suddenly the film night seemed less important and no one quite knew what to say.

'Sorry,' said Bella, 'I had no idea you had a baby sister who died.'

'No reason why you would,' said Tara breezily. 'Don't worry, it was quite a long time ago. It's not like it just happened. But anyway, I do various sponsored things to raise money for the hospital and I asked Mrs Frost if I could do a school quiz.'

'I love quizzes,' said Jasmine, clapping her hands and hugging Tara again.

The Fonteyn girls were all tired by the time they got back to the dorm, so they changed straight into their pyjamas and elbowed each other at the bathroom mirror in the battle to brush their teeth first.

'Yuk!' yelled Cassie, spitting violently into the sink. 'Washing-up liquid! Who did that?' Then she rolled her eyes, 'Stupid question. Bella!'

But Bella had already scuttled out of arm's reach.

'Oops, sorry! Must have got mixed up,' she called from the bedroom. 'Just thought we needed a bit of light-hearted fun to get us in the mood for the start of term.'

'Fun for you maybe,' said Cassie, furiously rinsing her mouth out. She turned to Bella with her hands on her hips: 'And what famous work of art did you steal *that* trick from, may I ask?'

'Oh no, that was all my own creation,' said Bella proudly. Megan was washing her face in the corner.

'Something I've always wondered about soap,' she mused to herself, 'is: can it ever be dirty? I mean if there's dirt on soap, you might say it's dirty, but then soap is cleanliness itself, so can it actually *be* dirty?'

Bella patted her on the head and gave her pitiful smile.

'Never mind, you'll get over it,' she said, and brusquely changed the subject. 'I liked your new friend, Jasmine. She was wearing Hollister jeans and a Jack Wills hoodie.'

'Was she?' said Jasmine. 'Is that good?'

'Well, it means she's got a sense of style, that's all,' answered Bella, settling back on her pillow.

'You're so shallow, Bella,' said Megan, yawning and stretching in her long Little House on the Prairie nightdress. 'Is that all you notice about people – their clothes labels?'

'Anyway, I guess we'll be seeing more of each other, if we're both going to be in *As You Like It*,' continued Bella sleepily, ignoring Megan's comment. 'Hey, maybe she'll lend me some of her clothes.'

By now, they were all in bed and even Bella was beginning to quieten down. Moments later, all the excitements of the first day back had faded away and the four were fast asleep.

Chapter 2: *Back in the Woods*

Bella was up before everyone else the next morning, and they awoke to see her sifting through the clothes in her drawer, giggling to herself.

'She's finally gone mad,' said Megan to the others as they began to surface, rubbing their eyes sleepily.

'Just you wait,' laughed Bella, 'I've got a great first trick up my sleeve – for Miss Flanders.'

'But I thought Miss Flanders was your favourite teacher,' said Jasmine. 'Why would you want to play a trick on her?'

'Well, that's exactly why – she's such a laugh. And she's too nice to get cross about it. Hold this a minute will you, Cassie,' she said, going over to her bed with a long ribbon.

Cassie held out her hand obligingly, still half asleep, and Bella bent her arm up at the elbow, with her hand resting on her shoulder, 'Now, tie my arm up, so that it looks like half an arm.'

Cassie did as she was told, the toothpaste incident having completely slipped from her mind during the night.

'That's right, tie it really tight so it looks like a stump.'

'Doesn't it hurt?'

'Yes, but it'll be worth it.'

Normally it was academic lessons in the morning and artistic disciplines in the afternoon, but on the first day back, the whole day was devoted to stage-work. So after breakfast, when the Fonteyn girls all said goodbye and went their separate ways, Bella strode off down the corridor to the drama studios, swinging her half-arm.

Miss Flanders was pretty in a glowing, healthy sort of way. She looked like one of those wooden dolls-inside-dolls, with rosy cheeks and bright sparkling eyes and shiny smooth hair. She walked into the classroom of excitable girls with a broad smile on her moony face, 'Good morning, you noisy lot. Anyone would think it was a school for chattering monkeys.'

'You mean it isn't?' joked Abigail, 'I think I might be in the wrong place then.'

Miss Flanders laughed along with everyone else and then started rooting through her bag for something. Books, tissues, lipsticks, pens and photos tumbled out of her bag and lay scattered about her as she wondered to herself, 'Oh, where is it for goodness' sake? I know it's in here somewhere. I had a great photo of mother and baby monkeys grooming each other,' she explained, 'and I was going to use for our first exercise, but never mind …'

She began to stuff all the scattered bits and pieces back into her bag and then clapped her hands for silence. They arranged themselves into a circle and sat down on the floor. That was when Miss Flanders first noticed Bella.

'Bella, my dear, what's happened to your arm?'

'Oh I lost it, Miss Flanders,' said Bella breezily, 'just after Christmas. I was chopping wood for the fire, you see –'

Miss Flanders' face had turned sheet-white and she was staring at Bella with open-mouthed horror.

'My dear, I'm so sorry!'

Big tears began to roll down her red apple cheeks and Bella couldn't carry on after that. She ran over to Miss Flanders and flung her good arm around her neck.

'Miss Flanders, it's only one of my silly jokes. My arm's fine,' and she tugged at the ribbon to let it down.

Miss Flanders looked annoyed and confused for a moment, and then her face broke into a smile.

'Well, I see you're in high spirits as ever, Bella. Someone has to be the clown, I suppose, and it might as well be you as anyone else. At least you mean no harm. Now, if you don't mind, we'll get on with the lesson.'

For their first drama activity they had to stand in a circle and when Miss Flanders pointed at a girl she had to say *'Why blame you me to love you?'* to someone else in the circle, then that girl had to say the same thing *'Why blame you me to love you?'* to someone else in the circle, and they had to say it to someone else, and so on. And each person had to try and say it in a different way – angrily, or sadly, or confusedly. Then they had to get into groups of three and invent a short scene, where one person was in love with one of the others, who was in love with the other one – a sort of love triangle where no one loved the one that loved them.

After that, Miss Flanders introduced them to the term's play: *As You Like It*.

'It's one of Shakespeare's best-loved comedies,' she said. 'Two girl cousins live in the royal court with the father of one, Duke Frederick, who has stolen the throne from the father of the other. Celia is the daughter of the Duke, Rosalind is his niece, the daughter of the brother he overthrew. Got it so far? So these girls are cousins – their fathers are brothers – and they live together, but are they friends or not?'

'Not,' most agreed. 'Their fathers are enemies.'

'Aha! Their *fathers* are enemies, yes, but the girls have grown up together and they adore each other – they are best, best friends. But then suddenly, after years of allowing his niece to live in the royal court, Duke Frederick decides to throw her out. What does his own daughter do when her cousin is thrown out of their home?'

'Goes with her too?'

'Exactly. They run away to a forest. And there's another pair of brothers at war with each other too, and the younger one, who's strong and good looking, runs away from his older brother who treats him cruelly, and ends up in the same forest. But we'll leave that for another day.'

By then it was break time. They went off to get their buns

and juice and stayed inside, huddled around the huge iron radiator in the dining hall, because it was too cold and gloomy outside. The drama girls were all in good moods – the first bit of acting of the term always warmed their hearts and everyone was glowing with enthusiasm. Even the icy, sharp sleet rapping angrily at the diamond window-panes couldn't dampen their cheerfulness.

'I'm going for Rosalind, definitely,' announced Bella.

'Well, I thought I would too, but maybe I'll go for Celia,' said Abigail. Lauren looked hurt.

'Then who would *I* be?' she whimpered. 'We agreed you were going to be Rosalind and I was going to be Celia.'

'Well, who knows who anyone's going to be?' said Abigail, putting her arm comfortingly around Lauren and giving her a squeeze. 'We haven't even auditioned yet, have we?'

When they got back after break they were put into pairs and they had half an hour to make up a short scene where two cousins run away from home. They had to think about why they were running away together, where they would go, and what they would do, and then just improvise the dialogue as they went along. Bella was paired with Abigail and they decided to make up a scene about two fashion-mad girls who were thrown out onto the streets of New York by their cruel aunt. They found an old factory warehouse full of rolls of fabric and they lived there with the mice, gradually stitching clothes they had designed out of the fabric and in the end becoming models. They knew it was a bit far-fetched but they had fun doing the New York accents and pretending to knock the nibbling mice off the cloth whilst they stitched clothes.

'Hey, we make a really good team,' said Abigail, 'hope we get paired up again.'

Miss Flanders was always very encouraging and she clapped enthusiastically at the end of their piece.

'Great!' she said, 'I loved that bit when she finds a mouse has nibbled a hole in her outfit, just as she is about to step on the catwalk. The girls in *As You Like It* have to be pretty resourceful too in order to survive life in the forest. But they have a different way of going about it – one of them dresses up as a boy and they rent a shepherd's cottage.'

At the end of the session, Miss Flanders gathered up her piles of papers and books and assorted props, and stuffed them into her bag.

'I'm going to start auditions at the end of the week,' she announced, 'so tomorrow I'll be giving out some scripts and we'll look through a couple of the key scenes, then you can decide which part to audition for. You are dismissed.'

And Miss Flanders left the room.

'Miss Flanders! Your bag!' sang a chorus of girls.

It was such a regular occurrence – she usually either slung someone else's bag over her shoulder, or left without one altogether – that they were used to having to call her back.

'That's not like me,' she said, as she picked up her bag and left again.

'She's a bit mad isn't she,' Abigail said to Bella as they were leaving the drama studio.

'Oh yes, completely, but we love her for it,' said Bella. 'The funny thing is, she's so forgetful, she forgets that she's forgetful and is always surprised when she loses something.'

* * *

Back in the dorm that night, as they were getting ready for bed, Bella told them all gleefully about how well her trick had worked.

'Poor Miss Flanders burst out crying,' she said, 'and I had to give in and show her I did have a whole arm after all. But it doesn't matter – it's all about that first moment of fooling them, you don't have to keep it up for long.'

'Well, I think you should watch it,' said Cassie, yawning and stretching as she began to take all the tiny red clips out of her short, springy hair, 'the teachers may get fed up if you keep on and on. Jokes aren't funny forever you know.'

'Oooh, listen to you Miss Goody-goody,' sang Bella. 'I remember a time when you were a bit of a law-breaker yourself. Don't tell me you've gone all Anne of Green Gables on us.'

Cassie knew that Bella was only joking, but she couldn't help feeling annoyed. She carried on getting ready for bed but a worm of irritation was niggling in her head, until finally she said, 'Anyway, I'm *not* a goody-goody. I've just grown up a bit.'

Jasmine came to her defence, 'Exactly. Cassie used to want to be all individual and, you know, like, her own person. But now she's got over it and she's happy to be like the rest of us.'

She smiled and put her arm around Cassie proudly.

'Not *exactly*,' Cassie prickled. 'I still am my own person.'

''Course you are,' said Bella provocatively, 'I bet you would still go out to the woods in the dark, after lights out.'

'Well I would if there was any reason to,' said Cassie, 'but there's no need to.'

Bella just raised her eyebrows in a maddening way and went to brush her teeth.

'Just ignore her,' said Megan, 'she's only trying to wind you up.'

But Cassie had been bitten.

'Well I *will* go out into the woods if it means so much to you,' she said when Bella came back in. 'I mean, if you really think I wouldn't go out into the woods right now, then I will.'

Bella shrugged, 'Well, you can if you like. I'm not recommending it or anything. I know the old Cassie would have done, but you know, if you'd rather just get into your nice warm bed and go to sleep …'

Every time Cassie turned her back, Bella would grin and wink at the others.

'Look Cassie, just ignore her,' said Megan again, 'you don't have to prove anything. Bella's just teasing you. *We* don't think you're a goody-goody.'

'No, I'm going,' replied Cassie with steely

determination. 'Bella obviously does and I want to show her she's wrong. I'll wait until after lights out.'

Cassie got into bed and pulled the covers up to her neck, buzzing with irritation. Maybe she *had* changed. Maybe she had turned into some kind of timid sheep without even realising it herself. It was certainly true that she would much rather just stay safely in bed. Would the old Cassie have done that? Had going to boarding school already changed her into a stupid puppet who did whatever she was told and couldn't think for herself? That had been her worst fear when she came to Starlight Academy – that she would lose her personality and just become a robot in a uniform. She pulled the covers up over her head and waited, with a deep frown on her face, for Miss Mackenzie, their housemistress, to come around at nine o'clock and say goodnight. She didn't *want* to go out into the woods at all, but she would have to now. She would never get to sleep otherwise: she would just lie there feeling annoyed not only with Bella, but with herself for being such a wimp.

Half an hour later, Cassie crept out of bed, pulled her trainers on and zipped up her thick puffa jacket over her pyjamas. Jasmine had already fallen asleep but Bella and Megan were still awake.

'Don't bother, Cassie,' Megan whispered, 'just go to sleep. Look, we all know you *would* dare to do it really. You don't have to actually do it.'

Bella was gleefully silent and Cassie, pulled on her hat

and gloves, 'See you in a while,' she whispered from the door, 'I'll bring you some chocolate from my secret hidey-hole up in that tree, just to prove that I've been there.'

She stepped as quietly as she could down the corridor and went slowly and silently down the stairs.

Once she was outside, she actually began to feel quite excited and pleased that she was doing this after all. It was exhilarating to be outside after dark – much more fun than being tucked up safely in bed. The air was sharp, the wind whistled in the trees, and black wisps of cloud rushed across the face of the moon. As soon as she was out of the back door, she began to run for the woods. She knew from previous experience that the back door by the sports changing rooms wasn't locked until 10.30 when Mr Burrows the maintenance man did his final rounds, so she would have to be quick to beat him there. She easily found the gap in the trees where she usually entered the woods and headed straight for her special climbing tree. She had found it in her first term at Starlight: it had a hole high up in the trunk, which she had used ever since as a secret store.

Normally Cassie was good at navigating, but it was very dark and one tree began to look much like another, and before long she realised that she was lost. Her heart lurched, but she tried not to panic. It was OK, she told herself. She still had time. She would forget about climb-ing the tree and just take a branch back or something as proof. Now all she had to do was get back to the gap in the trees. She stood still and tried to stay calm, then looked around her on all sides, doing a complete full turn and peering hard into the darkness. There were all sorts of gaps in the trees now that she really looked. How on earth would she ever know which one was hers? Her heart was thudding now and she felt furious with herself. How stupid – coming out here! What was she thinking? She was such an idiot, trying to prove to Bella that she wasn't a goody-goody. Who cared? She had proved herself more of a mindless puppet in falling for it than if she had just ignored her.

Terrified as she was, Cassie realised that she had to do something, she had to find her way out of the woods somehow, so she set off boldly in the direction towards which her instinct led her. She forgot all about taking a branch home with her and concentrated all her efforts instead on listening for any sound which might point her in the direction of school. She searched desperately in the night sky for any hint of a fuzzy brightness which might lead her towards the school buildings. But instead she came across an old shed – an old woodshed it looked like – standing in the middle of the woods. There were a couple of split logs on the ground inside and a headless axe had been propped up against the broken glass pane in one of the doors. She peered inside, curious in spite of her panic. There were two torn deck chairs stacked in the corner, and a tiny metal stove with a metal kettle on top. Amazing that she had never seen this place before, but when she thought about it, the woods were vast and she had only explored one small section. So where on earth was she then?

Suddenly out of the darkness there came the bark of a dog – it was Mr Burrows' dog, he must be on his locking-up rounds. Without thinking at all, she gave her whole attention to the sound and let it guide her through the woods. She ran faster than she had ever run before, hurtling through the trees towards the barking dog, desperate to get inside before the boot-room door got locked. It was still only 10.20, and that door was the last door on his rounds. Cassie knew where she was now, she could see the familiar gap in the trees – her gap – and beyond it the school, with its scattering of lights still on in upstairs windows. She didn't stop running until she almost smashed into the back door. She reached for the handle – it was open! – and she was inside. Cassie leant back against the inside of the closed door, gasping for breath, her heart hammering in her throat. She must be completely silent. She stood still for a few more moments and steadied her breath, then crept noiselessly up the stairs to her dorm. Safe at last! She reached out and turned the handle carefully, then pushed.

'Oh my god, you're in such trouble!' an anxious voice whispered from the darkness. 'Your dad phoned from America and they came to get you.'

Chapter 3: *Wilderness Club*

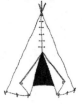

It turned out Cassie's dad had got his time differences muddled up and in his jet-lagged confusion, thought he was on the east coast of America where England is only five hours ahead, instead of on the west coast, where England is eight hours ahead. So he had called to speak to her at 9.45 pm, thinking it was 6.45 pm. Miss Mackenzie took pity on him and said she would go and see if Cassie was still awake, which was when all the trouble started. Mr Burrows' barking dog was not simply accompanying him on his normal nightly rounds, he was on the hunt for Cassie. By the time Cassie got back to the dorm, Bella was almost as scared as Cassie herself and was falling over herself to apologise, 'It's all my fault, Cassie, I'm so, so sorry. I was just teasing you for a laugh. I didn't really think anything bad would happen.'

By then Jasmine had woken up too and they all accompanied Cassie to Miss Mackenzie's room to say that she was safely back. Kind old Miss Mackenzie, who had worry-lines stretched across her forehead, didn't know whether to hug Cassie or shout at her.

'I thought you'd run away,' she said in a quiet voice, 'and I didn't know what to do. They told me you'd only gone out to the woods, but I didn't know what to believe.'

Cassie hardly slept for the rest of the night. She just lay there, twitching with worry. Mrs Frost didn't know anything about her night-time disappearance yet, but obviously Miss Mackenzie would have to tell her in the morning. How *could* she have been so stupid? Here she was starting off the second term just as she had started off the first – in trouble and probably grounded. And she had so wanted to leave all of that behind her.

Flo dashed into their dorm the next morning before breakfast, still in her pyjamas, with her hair flying all over the place.

'Has anyone got a spare school skirt?' she pleaded. 'Mum's gone and packed Tom's school trousers in my bag instead of my skirts. Hey, I wonder if Tom's walking around his school in one of my skirts? I doubt it somehow–'

They cut her short and filled her in on the night's dramas. Flo rushed over to Cassie, who was sitting ashen-faced on her bed, and gave her a hug.

'Oh, poor you! And just when you were getting over the whole rebel thing.'

Cassie wasn't sure that anyone's comments were making her feel any better. Bella vowed that she would accompany her to Mrs Frost's office straight after breakfast and was sure it wouldn't be as bad as she expected.

'I'm sure she'll be understanding,' agreed Flo, 'you know how she loves you.' Then she added apologetically, 'Um, skirt anyone? Sorry, in a bit of a hurry.'

Megan lent Flo a skirt and just as she was leaving, called out, 'Hey, are you going to audition to sing in *As You Like It*? Mr Swann said there were singing and instrumental parts too.'

'Yes, it's this afternoon isn't it? Let's go along together. See you later.' And she disappeared.

'You're so lucky,' said Cassie, 'all carefree, talking about auditions and singing and things. I've got nothing to even take my mind off it.'

'It'll be OK, I promise,' said Bella, giving her a hopeful smile. 'We'll think of some way of charming Mrs Frost. I think if we get to her first before she hears about it, we've got a better chance of winning her over.'

Bella and Cassie went straight to Mrs Frost's office after breakfast as planned. Cassie had brushed her hair as neatly as possible and was looking her smartest, and Bella was trying hard to look serious. It was proving difficult, however, because there was always a well of laughter bubbling inside her, waiting to burst out.

'I'm sorry,' she said to Cassie for the hundredth time, 'I'll try not to smile, I really will. I'll do my best humble and sorry face.'

Miss Mackenzie obviously hadn't reached Mrs Frost yet because she greeted them both with a smile.

'Good morning, you two, how can I help?'

'We'd like to talk to you Mrs Frost, please,' said Cassie, feeling sick.

'Well, I've only got a few minutes before assembly,' she said, consulting the neat, round watch which perfectly clasped her elegant wrist, 'but come into my office quickly.'

Bella was right: going to Mrs Frost before she was told of the night-time jaunt meant that she hadn't had time to get angry about it. But she certainly made up for lost time once they told her. The headmistress kept her eyes fixed on Bella whilst she explained what had led to Cassie's escapade, and confessed her own part in it, but as soon as she had finished, Mrs Frost turned to Cassie. It felt as if icicles were shooting out of her eyes, Cassie said afterwards.

'You know the rules, Cassie, and you've broken them. It's as simple as that.'

'The thing is,' said Cassie, on the edge of tears, 'before, I didn't mind much about getting into trouble, but now I really do. I just didn't think about it clearly.'

'Well, I understand that you were provoked,' Mrs Frost replied, 'but nonetheless, those are the very times when we must stand most firm. When this happened in your first term, I was willing to forgive your immaturity, but it is becoming something of a pattern. A pattern which cannot be allowed to continue.'

'I know,' said Cassie, 'and I'm really, really sorry. But please don't ground me because I'll just get so miserable with no outside world to distract me.'

Mrs Frost thought for a while and her gold bracelets clacked together as she tapped her well-manicured nails on the desk. Then she looked up at the clock.

'I haven't got time to discuss this properly at the moment,' she said, 'but let it be understood that you are on final warning, young lady. Unless you can think of some way to prove yourself worthy of my trust, I will have no choice but to ground you again. You are dismissed.'

She held open the door for the girls, and then whisked off down the corridor in the opposite direction, her helmet of immaculately brushed hair swishing slightly in the breeze but without a single strand slipping out of its assigned place.

* * *

Flo and Megan skipped down the corridor with arms linked, humming the same tune loudly and grinning from ear to ear. Just as they were about to go outside, they bumped into Cassie coming back in.

'What are you two looking so happy about?' asked Cassie miserably.

'We both got singing parts in *As You Like It*,' said Megan.

'*And* we're doing a flute duet,' added Flo. 'It will be like *The Meg and Flo Show*!' they giggled, thoroughly pleased with themselves.

'Anyway, where are you going?' asked Flo. 'Break's not over already is it?'

'No, not yet. It's just that I've had an idea and I wanted to try it out on a few people. See, I'm thinking of starting up a wilderness club, you know, to learn bushcraft skills.'

'*What* skills?' asked Megan with a bemused frown.

'Bushcraft.'

'Like cutting hedges in the shape of animals?' tried Flo. Megan nudged her.

'No, you idiot, it's a kind of fuzzy-felt thing, isn't it?'

'Maybe you too weren't the best people to ask,' muttered Cassie.

'Oh, I know what you mean,' offered Megan helpfully, 'skinning animals you've killed with a stick, that sort of thing.'

'Well not quite that,' said Cassie. 'More sort of making fires, and building camps in the woods, learning which berries are safe to eat – you know, survival skills.'

'Sounds lovely!' said Flo. 'Think I might stick to art club if you don't mind.'

Cassie went to see Mrs Frost after school and told her about her idea. She had spent a lot of time working out how best to phrase it, so that it sounded as if her motivation was all about offering something of benefit to the school. She outlined her plan – explained how they would meet one evening a week, and do some activities at the weekend – she had even found out during the course of the day that Mr Swann, the music teacher, was into hiking and outdoorsy stuff, so she suggested that he could be the teacher in charge.

'That way,' she finished, 'I can spend time outside, but in a legal way and I can show you that I can be responsible doing the things I love.'

Mrs Frost was suitably impressed. She almost allowed a smile to infiltrate her thin lips, but then she remembered her earlier threat and simply nodded her acceptance.

'Well, it all sounds very worthwhile and a good use of your free time. But remember, Cassie, you are standing on thin ice at this school and you must tread carefully. One false step and you're in deep water.'

As Cassie stood to attention in front of the headmistress, her fists clenched at her side, her nails digging into her palms, she couldn't help marvelling at how Mrs Frost always carried her comparisons through with exact precision to their logical conclusion – thin ice – tread carefully – deep water. She nodded vigorously to convey her complete understanding.

'Yes, Mrs Frost. I won't step out of line, I promise. I mean I won't step off the ice – or, you know, break the ice or anything.'

*   *   *

It was the final drama session of the day. Miss Flanders had finally found the little wooden recorder at the bottom of her bag and she began to play a folksy tune on it. Gradually the class quietened down to listen to her.

'Rosalind and Celia are in the forest now, but Rosalind has disguised herself as a boy called Ganymede. Also in the forest is Orlando, the younger brother who was bullied by his older brother and ran away. Remember Rosalind met him at the court when he beat the Duke's wrestler in a wrestling match. And she fell instantly in love with him. Now that they're in the same forest she's desperate to meet up with him.

But if she does meet him, there's a slight problem, isn't there?'

'She's dressed as a boy.'

'Exactly.'

Miss Flanders loved the story so much that her eyes shone with excitement as she told it, and everyone thought how pretty she looked.

'The first time Rosalind realises that Orlando is in the same forest as her is when she finds a love poem stuck to a tree. And it's a love poem to her. Wouldn't that be wonderful?' she smiled wistfully. 'Imagine being in a forest and finding a love poem addressed to you just stuck on a tree trunk. It would be so mysterious and magical.' She stared off into the distance and all the girls smiled. Then Bella's face suddenly lit up.

Chapter 4: *Poems on Trees*

By the time she reached the dorm after supper that night, Bella was bursting to share her brilliant plan.

'I've had the best idea!' she exploded.

'Uh-oh,' said Megan, without raising her eyes from her book, 'sounds dangerous.'

'No, wait! Listen to this one – you'll love it. It's not a trick exactly. Look, it's a long story, but basically poor Miss Flanders desperately needs some romance in her life and it's obviously our job to fix it, so I've got a plan. We write her some love poems and stick them on trees in the woods, you know, like in *As You Like It*, and then we take her out there to find them and she'll think she has a secret admirer. She'll be so happy.'

'Not if she doesn't *really* have a secret admirer she won't,' Jasmine pointed out sensibly.

'Ah, well that's the challenge. We have to find her one. But the question is – who can be her secret admirer?'

'Mr Swann,' said Cassie, without another moment's thought.

All heads turned in her direction, so she explained how she had gone to see Mr Swann about the wilderness club and he had been telling her how he loved to go walking and climbing, and how one of the best times of his life was walking up Mount Kilimanjaro in Africa, staying in mountain huts on the way.

'Anyway, he looked a bit sad when he said that, considering it was meant to be one of the best times of his life, so I asked, "*Did you walk up the mountain all on your own?*" and he said yes, he did, and I said, "*That must have been a bit lonely*," and he agreed and said, "*Yes, it would have been nice to have someone to share it with, I suppose.*" And straightaway I thought, poor Mr Swann, he's got terrible shoes but he deserves some love in his life.'

'Perfect!' shrieked Bella clapping her hands. 'Mr Swann it is! Now, let's get on with the poems and I can post them up in the woods during break tomorrow morning.'

Everyone was so pleased with the idea of bringing Miss Flanders and Mr Swann together that they all jumped onto Bella's bed, while Megan got some paper out of her desk. But before Megan had even got the lid off her pen, Jasmine suddenly sang out:

'*My heart is aflame, Miss Flanders, when I hear your name, I hope that one day when you see me you will feel the same –*'

They looked at her, amazed.

'Wow, Jasmine!' gasped Megan, 'Did you think that up just now?'

'Of course!' said Jasmine, laughing. 'It's not as if I spend my spare time secretly making up love poems from one teacher to another. I'm not *that* sad.'

'Go on, do some more,' said Bella, nudging her with her elbow.

Megan scribbled away, and they all watched awestruck, as Jasmine reeled off:

'My heat skips a beat, Miss Flanders, when I see your face, It's the prettiest face I've ever seen, on earth or in outer space.

Wait, I'm not sure about that one, it sounds like he's saying she's prettier than an alien which is not such a great compliment, but I'll keep going and we can always go back and change it.'

'Jasmine and her hidden talents!' said Cassie, 'Remember the gingerbread teacher competition? I wonder what else she can do.'

Jasmine grinned and carried on:

'My heart will break, Miss Flanders, if I cannot be with you, So tell me now, oh tell me now, if you will love me true.'

Jasmine sat back and sighed with satisfaction and the others all clapped and whooped.

Bella rushed off to Miss Mackenzie's room to ask for a tea-bag (she said it was for an art project) and they crumpled up the sheet of paper, then dabbed it with the wet tea-bag to make it look like an ancient brown scroll.

'Now, perhaps two more would be enough,' said Bella in a business-like manner, 'Ready Jasmine? Got your pen Megan? Right, off we go.'

'Your eyes are brighter than the stars, Your hair shines

like the … like the … wait a minute,' said Jasmine, pausing mid-poem, 'how is she going to know they're from Mr Swann?'

'Hmm, good point.' Bella scratched her head in thought. 'I know, we'll do a swan design at the bottom of each poem, as a hint. She'd be crazy not to work it out. Now, what does her hair shine like?'

* * *

As soon as they were let outside at break the next morning, Bella dashed off to the woods, the poems clutched in her hand. It was a beautiful spring morning, bright with pale sunshine. The birds were singing their hearts out and there was something about the first few crocuses popping their heads out of the ground that made everyone feel mad with excitement. The whole world felt full of hope and bursting with happiness, and the thought of Miss Flanders finding love poems on the trees just seemed so perfectly matched to the day. Bella returned a few minutes later, panting and red-faced, but looking thoroughly pleased with herself.

'Done!'

'Done what?' asked Abigail, joining the group of Fonteyn girls, with her faithful follower Lauren at her side. They even walked the same way – a sort of cowboy swagger – and every time Abigail flicked her sideways fringe out of her eyes, Lauren did the same.

'Oh, I had this great idea about Miss Flanders,' explained Bella breathlessly. 'We've written her some love poems and hung them on trees in the woods. You know, like in *As You Like It*. Now we just have to get her to go down to the woods and find them.'

'Love poems? From *you*?'

'Yeah, right!' laughed Bella. 'No, love poems from a secret admirer. Look I'll explain later, in drama this afternoon.'

'Anyway, listen,' said Abigail to Bella, as if no one else was around, 'my dad's just told me he's got extra tickets to the premiere of *Wild Thing*. He says I can bring someone and I was thinking – do you want to come? We'd get to go to the cast party afterwards too.'

'Do I want to come?' squealed Bella, so loudly that she didn't hear Lauren's gasp of shock. 'Of course I want to come!'

Lauren let out a yelp, like a puppy who's had its tail trodden on: 'Abi!'

Abigail put an arm around her, 'Look, it's in half-term – you're going to pony school, aren't you?'

Lauren nodded, but the look of abject misery didn't leave her face.

'Half-term?' echoed Bella, and her face fell. 'Oh.' She looked nervously across at Megan and then said to Abigail, 'I'll talk to you about it later, OK?'

Just then, the bell rang and the Year 7s and 8s parted to go to their separate lessons. Cassie sighed heavily, 'It would be alright if it was a quick sort of lesson, but history always feels so dreadfully *long*,' she moaned.

'I know,' agreed Jasmine. 'It's because Mr Lockwood takes so long to say everything, and uses such long words. It feels like a never-ending blurb of historicalness.'

Mr Lockwood took history very seriously and was constantly baffled that everyone else didn't feel the same. If you didn't know some tiny detail about a topic, he was amazed that you didn't want to find out immediately.

Their current topic was the Industrial Revolution in Victorian times, and just the sound of the phrase 'industrial revolution' made Cassie want to fall asleep. Mr Lockwood was writing something up on the white-board in a squeaky pen and they were supposed to be copying down the title, but the sun was streaming in through the window and it felt like there were far more interesting things going on somewhere else. Cassie grinned across at Jasmine and did a hand-puppet of a swaying swan's neck as a reminder of their secret plan. Mr Lockwood happened to turn around at that moment and saw her.

'Instead of doing a disco dance, Cassie March, perhaps you can tell us what major change the Industrial Revolution brought about within our nation?'

He stopped and stared at her with his hands on his hips. He was trying not to look too pleased with himself for having identified that she was doing a 'disco dance'. Cassie looked blank. She didn't understand the question let alone know the answer. She looked around the classroom, hoping to find the answer on a poster somewhere, but no such luck. She must at least sound as if the industrial revolution was important to her, or he would get even more offended.

'Um, a revolutionary sort of change?' she said hopefully.

Mr Lockwood stared at her with a disappointed frown.

'It's all very well to joke,' he said in a hurt tone, 'but what do you think your life would be like today if the industrial revolution hadn't happened?'

Another question that it was actually impossible to answer.

'I'm not sure,' she said, trying her best to sound as if she really cared quite deeply about this. 'It would be less revolutionary?'

Mr Lockwood pointed his pen at her and said irritably, 'I'll tell you what it would be like, Cassie March. You would be living on a farm, working from dawn til dusk, tilling the soil, boiling vegetables that you had pulled from the earth over a smoky fire, and bedding down next to your animals on the ground, day in day out until you died. No school, no books, no dance lessons for you.'

He turned back to the board with a look of satisfaction at the bleak picture he had created.

'And certainly no epods,' he said, delighted that he had remembered the word for them at last.

Then he started drawing pictures on the board – a steam-train, a telephone, a camera and a light-bulb.

'Now, choose one of these objects on the board, please. Any one. And draw it at the top of your page. Then start to think about what it enables us to do. Write a bullet-pointed list, and then move on to the next one. Just to start you off, a telephone for example allows us to '*communicate with friends*' – something you all never tire of doing, I'm sure.'

There was a sniffle from Lauren's desk as she gazed mournfully at Abigail. Mr Lockwood looked puzzled again for a moment but then shook his head and decided not to get involved.

By the time afternoon lessons had started, the sense of general excitement was buzzing around the school, and the drama girls were doing acrobatics all over the place when Miss Flanders arrived.

'Ah! Spring,' said Miss Flanders, breezing into the room with a huge smile on her face. 'Always does this to girls. I know – let's all do some springing and get it out of our systems.'

She joined in the cart-wheeling and side-skipping and jumps and leaps for a few moments, and when they were all red-faced and breathless, she got them to sit in a circle on the floor.

'Now, auditions start tomorrow, so today we will do some group work on a couple more scenes before I assign parts and we start rehearsals in earnest. Today, we meet two new characters in the woods, a shepherd and shepherdess. He is madly in love with her but she isn't remotely interested in him. And the ruder she is to him, the more he loves her. But when this shepherd-ess – called Phoebe – meets Rosalind (dressed up as Ganymede, remember) she falls head-over-heels in love with 'him'. And the ruder Rosalind is to Phoebe, in an attempt to put her off, the more Phoebe loves her. So that's the scene we're going to work on today – the hopeless love triangle.'

Miss Flanders put them in pairs and got them to improvise scenes between the shepherd who loved the shepherdess who didn't love him back. Then she handed out scripts and gave them some time to read over the scene and prepare a version of it, before calling on various pairs to present their versions.

At the end of the session, they were all still full of energy, and were gabbling away and giggling so much that Miss Flanders sent them off to run two laps of the hockey pitches. Bella seized her moment and hung back whilst the others jogged out of the room complaining loudly.

'Miss Flanders,' she said, smiling sweetly.

'What is it Bella? Lost a leg this time?'

'What? Oh yes, that, sorry about that. No, this is nothing like that. The thing is, a few of us were thinking that it would be so amazing to do this play in the woods. You know, instead of in the school theatre. And, well, we think we've found the perfect spot and we just wanted to show you it.'

A smile crept across Miss Flanders' face and she whispered to Bella, 'You know, it's funny because I've been thinking the same thing myself.'

'So will you come and see the place, after school today?'

'Alright then, I don't see why not. And perhaps we can talk to Mrs Frost about your idea.'

*   *   *

48

A small group of girls accompanied Miss Flanders into the woods that evening. There was still half an hour before dinner and the sun hadn't yet started to set. The sky was a bruised purple and there was a chill in the air, but they were all well wrapped up and they sang as they walked, with arms linked, down to the woods. Abigail was with Bella and Miss Flanders at the front, while Megan, Jasmine, Cassie and Flo followed close behind. Lastly came Lauren, sulking and refusing to walk with anyone else. She didn't really want to come at all, but still couldn't help herself from going wherever Abigail went. At last, they got to a clearing in the trees – the random site which Bella had picked earlier that day – and Bella held out her arms to announce it.

'Ta da!'

There was nothing special about it that made it perfect for a theatre, because of course that had never been the point, so Miss Flanders looked about her in some confusion at first.

'It might be a bit far from school, Bella dear. I mean, we'd have to bring the set and the props and things …'

A few fat drops of rain fell and Miss Flanders looked up at the sky anxiously.

'We must get back to school,' she said, and then, checking her watch, 'oh my goodness, look at the time! We can talk about your idea tomorrow Bella, but I'm not sure this is really the right spot anyway.'

Bella was getting desperate. The plan was about to be ruined. She gasped, 'Wait a minute, what's that?'

'What's what?' asked Miss Flanders impatiently, looking at her watch again.

'Over there on the tree.'

Miss Flanders looked off into the distance where Bella was pointing.

'Looks like a notice pinned to the tree. Perhaps someone has lost something. A cat or something. Let's have a quick look.'

They hung back and let Miss Flanders approach the tree on her own. They watched how she slowed down as she got closer, and then peered at the sheet of paper, and then took it down and read it properly, a hesitant smile slowly spreading across her face. Then she turned around and looked at them. She was trying to be disapproving, but she couldn't help smiling.

'What is it Miss Flanders?' asked Bella innocently.

'You know exactly what it is – love poems on trees, to me,' said Miss Flanders, shaking her head, but still smiling.

'Who from?' asked Abigail, with perfect incomprehension.

'Well, it's *you*, girls, of course. I know *that*. But it's lovely nonetheless. Just as lovely as I thought it would be, to find a poem addressed to oneself on a tree. And very sweet of you.'

'It's not us!' they all protested loudly over and over again, 'Wow! I wonder who they're from Miss Flanders. Hey, maybe there's a hint somewhere – have a look.'

Although it was raining quite hard by now, no one

had paid it much attention, until Miss Flanders, who was clutching the bunch of poems, suddenly noticed that the ink was beginning to run. She looked up at the sky in surprise, then looked at her watch again and gasped, 'Oh my goodness, come on girls!'

She had stopped smiling now and her voice was stern.

'It's time to go. We're drenched and we're going to be late for dinner.'

They all ran back to school, Miss Flanders in the lead still holding the poems. The corridors were alarmingly quiet when they crashed, dripping and laughing, through the front door. Miss Flanders shushed them and they stopped to listen. The clatter and chatter of dinner in full flow was leaking out of the dining hall. Miss Flanders' face was pale and drawn. She nodded her head towards the door, 'Come on, then. We'll just have to face the music.'

She led them into the dining hall, her eyes trained on the floor, hoping that somehow their entrance would not be noticed, but the entire school looked towards the doorway as the soaking wet bunch trooped in. A hush fell over the room and all eyes moved from the dripping huddle to Mrs Frost. Mrs Frost was the first to break the silence.

'You'd better go and get dry,' she said in a cold, disapproving tone. 'You too Miss Flanders. I'll have to ask the kitchen staff to keep some dinner warm for you.'

They turned to leave the room and she added in a quieter voice, 'It's most unfortunate, as they were hoping to get home early tonight because of the weather conditions.'

Outside the room, Miss Flanders gave the girls an 'oops' look and whispered, 'I don't think Mrs Frost is very pleased with me.'

*   *   *

That night, as the Fonteyn girls were drifting off to sleep, tired after all the excitement in the rain, there was a knock at the bedroom door. They all sat up and Jasmine gasped, wide-eyed, 'Who can it be?'

'Who is it?' called Megan in a loud whisper

'It's me, Abi. I need to talk to Bella.'

Bella hopped out of bed and went to the door. Abigail didn't look her usual confident self. There was a crease of worry across her forehead.

'It's about the auditions,' she whispered, 'I need your help desperately.'

'Sure, what is it?'

'Look, I've been really dumb,' Abigail confessed, 'I haven't learnt my lines for the auditions tomorrow and I really, really want to get the part of Celia. Can you help me? Please?'

'Of course,' said Bella, delighted to be so needed.

Megan huffed impatiently and said, 'Hey, you guys, can you go out into the corridor if you're going to be yakking. We need to get some sleep.'

So Bella and Abigail slipped out into the splintery, draughty corridor and closed the door.

Chapter 5: *Quiz Night*

It was Friday night and Cassie, Flo, Jasmine, Bella and Megan had all piled into Piaf, Abigail and Lauren's dorm. They had half an hour to kill before Tara's fundraising quiz, and since they had had to postpone their private film night, Abigail had invited the Fonteyn girls round to Piaf. Flo had come along too because her other room-mates weren't about – Tara was busy setting up the quiz, Daisy was practising in a music room somewhere, and Freya was off being grumpy in the library. It was the first time they had been in any other dorm apart from Fonteyn or Hepburn, and Piaf was a revelation to them. It was a dorm in two halves: one extremely messy and plastered from floor to ceiling with film posters, the other alarmingly tidy, with bare walls except for a neat line of sports medals hung up on hooks.

'Did half of the room get hit by a hurricane or something?' Cassie asked as they came in.

On Abigail and Lauren's half of the room, there were layers of clothes not only piled high on chairs but scattered all over the floor, there were CD and DVD cases lying open on every free surface, half-buried under a layer of sweet wrappers, and magazines papered the beds.

'How do you get away with it?' asked Jasmine, hor-rified and awestruck in equal measure. 'Hasn't your housemistress been in for ages?'

'This is just today's mess,' replied Abigail casually. 'It's OK, we'll do something about it before she comes round later.'

'But who lives in the other half of the room?' asked Cassie. 'Poor them, whoever they are.'

'Oh they're sports freaks,' replied Lauren, 'hardly ever here. You know Antonia, the one who's captain of everything going, and another Year 8 girl called Katie who's equally sporty.'

'I know Antonia,' said Megan, 'she's a singer in our year. Katie's a dancer, isn't she?'

'Yes,' said Cassie, 'and Antonia beat me in the tennis tournament last term remember.'

'Well, they spend all of their time outside playing sport,' said Abigail, 'so they only ever come in here to sleep. Or to change clothes,' she added, 'and they do that so quickly you hardly have a chance to say Hi before they've gone again.'

Bella was still ecstatic about getting the part of Rosalind in the *As You Like It* auditions that morning, and she and Abigail – who had got the part of Celia thanks to Bella's help – were dancing around in celebration, much to the secret annoyance of everyone else. Lauren was slumped miserably on the floor, flicking through a magazine without reading it at all. She had got the part of Corrin the old shepherd, and was Celia's understudy. Jasmine pursed her lips and clasped her hands behind her back in a desperate attempt to stop herself from tidying up. She was longing to get to work on the room, but didn't want to look like a complete granny by folding up all their clothes and putting them in drawers. In order to calm her twitching hands, she went over to the window and surreptitiously straightened the bunched-up curtains.

In truth, Jasmine was beginning to wish she hadn't met these two in the holidays and brought them in to upset the happy world of the Fonteyn girls. They had all been great friends before and now everything seemed a bit less shiny and felt a bit less comfortable.

'You should see the view from our room,' she said proudly from the window, 'we can see the sea sparkling in the distance.'

'Whereas we just get the muddy old hockey pitches,' moaned Abigail.

'But *you* get to see the woods,' said Cassie enviously.

'You and your woods!' said Flo, 'she's always going on about them. Have you heard that she's even going to set up some club where you kill animals and eat acorns in the woods. Sounds fun, doesn't it?'

Everyone laughed and Cassie came to her own defence: 'But there's just something so mysterious and exciting about woods. It always feels as if some kind of adventure is about to happen. If this was my room, I'd probably sit at the window all day looking into the woods through binoculars, just to see if anything secret was going on.'

'And the highlight of your day would be when a leaf fell off a tree,' teased Flo.

'Well *I'm* joining your wilderness club anyway,' said Bella. 'It sounds fab.'

'Me too,' agreed Abigail enthusiastically.

'But Abi,' said Lauren in a pleading voice, 'we hate outdoorsy stuff. We hate insects and mud and everything like that, remember?'

'I don't,' said Abigail dismissively, 'not any more.'

'Well I'm sorry, but you can count me out,' said Flo. 'I can't think of anything worse.' Jasmine and Megan agreed.

'I'd rather read a book about adventures in the woods than actually have any,' Megan decided firmly

Abigail suddenly remembered something and darted over to her bedside table.

'Hey Bella! I got you something to say thanks for re-hearsing my lines with me.'

She rifled through piles of magazines, CDs and DVDs and then pulled out a large photograph triumphantly.

'Here it is!'

She handed it to Bella. It was a signed photo of Jed Brogan, the star of *Wild Thing*. He had scrawled 'For Bella, with love' across his face. Bella nearly fainted with pleasure.

'How?' she gasped. It was all she could manage to say.

'My Dad. I got him to ask Jed to do it for you.'

'But how?' she gasped again.

'I called him this morning and asked him to courier it over. It's no big deal.'

'I can't believe you got that for me, Abi,' Bella shrieked. 'It's the coolest thing I've *ever* had. I will love it forever and ever.'

She gave her a massive hug.

'Well, I couldn't have done that audition without you,' shrugged Abigail. 'You were a star, thanks.'

Just then, Antonia and Katie burst into the room, red-faced and laughing.

'I easily won,' said Antonia, 'and I wasn't even particularly trying.'

'Yeah, well your legs are like twice as long as mine. I was much faster, and if I'd had your legs stuck on to me *I* would easily have won.'

'Whatever!' said Antonia, giving her a final friendly push and suddenly noticing the rest of the room. 'Hey, you two had better tidy up. It's the quiz in five minutes and Miss Hurley will be coming round for room inspection straight after.'

Antonia and Katie were complete opposites: Antonia was tall and muscular and strikingly beautiful, with skin that shone like brand-new chestnuts and deep brown eyes. Katie was small and skinny, with pale, almost translucent skin that burnt easily, and bright green eyes. They both had short hair – Antonia's twisted into lots of tiny knots and Katie's blonde and spiky – and they

both lived for sport. They shot around the room, grab-
bing their wash bags and a bundle of clean clothes, and
they were both showered and dressed before Abigail and
Lauren had even begun to pick up any of their mess.

'Time for the quiz,' announced Antonia, heading for
the door.

'Look, you lot go ahead,' said Jasmine, 'I'll stay back
and tidy the room. I'm desperate to anyway and it won't
take me long.' And she shooed them out of the door.

* * *

When they reached the dining hall, Tara was whisking
about efficiently with a clipboard clutched to her chest
and a pen behind her ear, as if she was organizing the
Oscars. There were four tables set out at the top of the
hall, one for each of the four school houses: Coliseum,
Sadler's Wells, Adelphi and Lyric. In the middle of each
table in front of the captain's chair sat a push-bell, a
sheet of paper and a pen. There was a chair each side
of the captain where the other team members would sit
and a glass of water at each place. Tara had chosen Mr.
Lockwood the history teacher to be quiz-master, and had
arranged for spotlights to be rigged up, bathing both the
quiz master and each of the four captains in an individual
pool of light. The rest of the hall was plunged into darkness, so that as the audience entered there were several
bangs and trips and ouches and giggles. The effect, as
planned, was very dramatic and the contestants immediately felt nervous and wished they hadn't put their names
forward. Each contestant had paid £5 to enter the quiz,

and the triumphant team would win £50 worth of clothes vouchers each, donated by one of the big stores in town. The audience members had each paid £1 to watch the quiz, and they would all be entered into a raffle to win various other prizes donated by local shops.

When the shuffling and chatting and knocking into things in the dark reached a crescendo, Tara pinged one of the bells several times to call for silence. She signalled with a business-like wave for Mrs Frost to come forward, and the headmistress addressed the school from the front: 'Welcome, girls, to the Starlight Quiz in aid of Riverside Children's Hospital. As some of you may know, Tara Davenport has been raising money for this thoroughly worthwhile cause for some years now, since the death of her baby sister who was beautifully cared for at Riverside. This quiz is just one of many events she has organized to raise money for a special play-garden in the hospital grounds, which Tara has asked to be named the Starlight Garden. Tara has devised the quiz herself and it promises to be tremendous fun. I must say, I can't think of a better way for you all to spend Friday night. So – enjoy!'

There were cheers and whistles and applause all round as Tara stepped forwards, squeezed into a tight velvet dress, with high heels that made her look more like twenty-one than twelve. She took the microphone with a charming smile and a flick of her hair before announcing, 'Thank you all for coming. The first round of tonight's quiz will consist of questions about books, music and films, the second is sports and news, as I think it is very important to keep up to date with what is going on in the world. Are you ready Mr Lockwood? Then let the quiz begin, and may the best team win!'

Cassie sat at the Adelphi table with Abigail and another Year 7 girl called Zoe; Flo sat at the Sadler's Wells table with Megan and a Year 7 girl called Willow. Bella was captain of the Lyric table with Jasmine and Lauren at her side, and at the Coliseum table were Antonia, and Flo's other roommates, the eccentric Daisy and the grumpy Freya. Sadler's Wells were glad to have Megan for the books round, and Coliseum had Antonia for the sport and Daisy for the music. Adelphi's only real hope was Abigail for her knowledge of films, which could only be rivalled by Bella on the Lyric team. As predicted, Sadler's Wells sailed into the lead in the first round, with Megan able to answer almost every literary question and Flo most of the music ones. Willow didn't seem to know very much about anything; she just sat there smiling nervously, unable to press the buzzer and looking as if she was about to cry. But Bella and Abigail knew most of the film questions between them, and Zoe was bookish too, so towards the end of the round, Adelphi began to catch up with Sadler's Wells. There were a few questions which nobody knew the answer to and then Mr Lockwood would shake his head in puzzled disbelief and say, 'Come on, surely *someone* knows this one. It's very well-known.'

He could never understand other people's ignorance.

It came to the final question of the round, and Adelphi were still a few points behind when Mr Lockwood read out: 'In which country was this season's blockbuster *Wild Thing* filmed?'

Cassie grinned and raised her eyebrows at Abigail, waiting for her to press the buzzer and answer the question. But Abigail just sat there, here eyes flicking nervously from side to side, and did nothing. Cassie gave her a nudge and whispered, 'Go on.'

But Abigail just elbowed her back and hissed, 'Go on yourself!'

Finally, Bella pressed the buzzer and said, 'I'm pretty sure it was Mexico.'

'Mexico is correct. Three points to Lyric.'

In the second round, Antonia answered every question on sport. Before any of the others even had time to open their mouths, her hand shot to the buzzer at the speed of a bullet. And then Freya, who was slumped in her chair behind a curtain of black hair, proved to be a genius on current affairs. She answered every single question in the News round, reaching out to press the buzzer without shifting position or smiling. She didn't even look pleased when she got an answer right, she just waited for the next question. Mr Lockwood had to keep asking her to repeat herself, as she mostly spoke down to the table, but since nobody else knew the answers anyway, she easily won the round for Coliseum, who eventually won the whole quiz. Afterwards, Cassie went up to her to congratulate her, 'Wow – you know a lot of stuff about things! I had no idea.'

'Well, someone has to take an interest in the real world outside this stupid fairytale castle,' she replied and walked away.

Freya was a gifted musician in Year 7 who shared Hepburn dorm with Flo, Daisy and Tara, but ever since she had arrived at Starlight Academy she had been in a bad mood. Nothing anyone said could lift her out of it, and nobody knew what the problem was, although occasionally she would suddenly seem cheerful and normal, just for a moment, before slinking back to her den of gloom.

After the quiz, as they were milling about drinking hot chocolate and waiting for the raffle prizes to be drawn, Bella nudged Abigail and said,

'Sorry I beat you to that *Wild Thing* one. I was kind of waiting for you to get it but you were taking ages so I decided to buzz.'

'Yeah, how come you didn't answer that one?' said Cassie. 'I thought your dad was a director on that film. We could have won that round.'

Abigail shot Cassie a withering look.

'Well, *sorreee* that I don't exactly remember every tiny detail of my parents' lives,' she said. 'I do have a life of my own, you know.'

'I can't believe Antonia has got all those clothes vouchers,' wailed Bella. 'What a waste! She'll probably just spend them on a mountain of sports socks or something!'

Then she spotted Miss Flanders over the other side of the hall.

'*Try to see if any looks pass between them,*' she had instructed the others at the beginning of the evening. But none had, and now she decided to take a more direct approach to her matchmaking.

'Miss Flanders,' she called out, skipping over to her and then adding in a whisper, 'have you found out yet who the poems were from?'

'Oh shush!' said Miss Flanders, her face flushing. 'I know it was just another one of your tricks.' Then she confided behind her hand, 'Mrs Frost wasn't very pleased with me about that whole episode. But I must say it was worth it for the fun of it all. It's not every day one finds a love poem to oneself on a tree.'

Chapter 6: *The Arrival of Miss Spitzer*

As soon as they walked into assembly on Monday morning, they could tell that something was not right. When they talked about it afterwards, they all said how the room had an unnatural hush to it, and seemed cold and gloomy. The teachers were lined up on the stage as usual and at first it all looked normal until Cassie noticed two things: firstly, that there was an extra teacher whom she had never seen before, and secondly that Miss Flanders seemed to be crying. Her head was bent towards her lap and she kept holding a tattered tissue up to her nose. It wasn't long before all was revealed. After they had sung the school song, and a girl from Year 11 had read out a long poem that she had written, Mrs Frost addressed the school: 'Now, girls, we are delighted to welcome to our school a visiting teacher from America. Miss Spitzer comes to us from a top girls' school in New York and she will be teaching drama whilst Miss Flanders takes some leave due to personal circumstances. We are of course all very sad to be losing Miss Flanders,' she smiled what seemed a fake smile across at her, 'if only for a short time. But we are extremely fortunate to have in Miss Spitzer such a worthy replacement. So, girls, please join me in extending a warm welcome to Miss Spitzer from New York.'

Mrs Frost began to clap and a few others joined her, until gradually it built up into a weak, ragged round of applause. The drama girls, who adored Miss Flanders, were in too deep a state of shock to even lift their hands.

Then Miss Spitzer stood up. She was wearing three-quarter length shorts, with a sharp line ironed down the front. Beneath her long shorts were some tanned, smooth legs, and then a pair of bright white socks and bright white trainers, both as blinding as her teeth when she smiled. She wore a tight, baby-pink fleece and her blonde hair was held back by sunglasses. She didn't look at all shy to be addressing the school for the first time, in fact she walked up to the front centre of the stage and stood right in front of Mrs Frost, blocking her from view.

'Thank you, Miz Frost. It's a pleasure to be here at Starlight Academy,' she said in her clipped New York accent, somehow making the name of the school sound so much cooler than they had ever thought it before. 'It's a ril privilege to be teaching at such a prestigious and historic English school – an opportunity for which I thank my lucky stars.' She stopped and grinned because it was meant to be a joke but no one noticed until it was too late, so she went straight on, her voice hard and nasal, 'Now I'm sure you're all greatly saddened to be losing your darling Miss Sanders, but I hope we'll all have a whole bunch of fun together.'

Miss Spitzer flashed her perfect white teeth and there were several suspicious looks from the crowd of girls. In their experience, teachers who talked about having a lot of fun usually weren't much fun.

'And in the meantime,' she trammelled on, 'Miss Sanders will take some quality emotional recuperation.'

Whispers of *some what?* passed around the room and the general consensus was that she was involved in some kind of secret operation to do with the qulity of chicken coops.

As they filed out of the assembly hall, Cassie saw that Bella's face was ashen. She went over to try and cheer her up, 'Hey, it's not forever. She's not leaving, just taking a break.'

'It's all my fault,' said Bella, staring blankly into space.

'How come?' asked Cassie, genuinely confused.

'Well, it's obvious isn't it? Miss Flanders has been sacked. Because of the whole coming out to the woods in the rain thing. Oh poor Miss Flanders! Don't you remember how Mrs Frost looked at her when we all came in? She was already thinking then how to get rid of her.'

'Are you sure? Mrs Frost did say she was just taking a break for personal reasons.'

'Of course she did. What else could she say? Oh, *why* did I have to come up with that stupid plan? Now, instead of finding Miss Flanders a boyfriend, I've lost her her job. What an idiot!'

Cassie tried to persuade Bella that she might be wrong, but she was inconsolable. As far as she was concerned, it was obvious: Mrs Frost was angry with Miss Flanders for messing about instead of being a sensible teacher, and she had decided to get rid of her. Bella was heartbroken.

* * *

The first meeting of the Wilderness Club was held after school on Monday. All the Fonteyn and Hepburn girls went along to support Cassie, even Megan, Flo and Jasmine, who had no interest in learning how to survive in the wilderness. But there was something about the first days of spring that no one could resist, and they all felt unaccountably cheerful. The sticky buds on the trees had just exploded tiny green leaves, the ground was speckled with primroses – like clusters of stars which had been hibernating underground all winter – and there was that fresh smell of brand new life in the air, which made everything feel possible.

'I just love evening birdsong,' trilled Flo with a beaming smile. 'I think it's even better than in the morning because it's like they're giving it their last blast before bedtime.'

Abigail raised her eyes at Bella as if to say 'W*hat a weirdo*!'

'OK, whatever!' she said. 'Can't say I've ever noticed birdsong much – I mean not enough to make a speech about it or anything.'

'You've never noticed birds singing?' said Flo, wide-eyed. 'Are you deaf or something?'

'No, just kind of got more interesting things to think about.'

By then they had reached a clearing in the woods and Cassie, who was brimming with excitement, turned around to face them all: 'OK everyone, thanks for coming. I think we're all going to have a "whole bunch of fun" at the Wilderness Club. With the help of Mr Swann, we're going to learn all sorts of bushcraft techniques, like how to start a fire without matches, and how to keep it going and how to find food out in the wild. We'll also learn how to make a natural shelter, and how to make tools for hunting, and how to trap animals. I'm not sure if we'll actually hunt or trap anything – '

'No, because it's illegal,' Mr Swann interrupted.

'And cruel,' added Flo.

'And disgusting,' agreed Megan.

'OK, OK,' said Cassie, 'but anyway it's going to be so cool. And one weekend, Mrs Frost has agreed that we can camp out in the woods overnight.'

'But why would we want to do that?' asked Flo, genuinely mystified.

'Oh Flo, you have absolutely no sense of adventure,' moaned Cassie, 'anyway, today's session is all about fire. And first Mr Swann is going to demonstrate how to create fire by friction using a bow drill. I can't wait!' Cassie rubbed her hands in excitement.

Mr Swann was, on the surface of it, seriously square. He had no dress sense at all, and for the first session of Wilderness Club was wearing a green waterproof hat which had zipped pockets all over it and clung to his skull, brown cords that were too short for him and were pulled up too high, and a mustard-yellow waxed jacket with thousands more zipped pockets in it. But he was so square that he was almost cool.

'This is called a bow-drill,' he announced proudly, holding up a long wooden bow which he had bent out of a peeled stick. 'It is one of the earliest methods of starting a fire.'

He looped the bow's string around a stick, which was stuck in a hole in a piece of wood on a cloth, then proceeded to move the bow backwards and forwards so that the stick turned in the hole. There were a few false starts, and it took some patience, which some of the girls lacked – Abigail in particular started looking at her watch and whispered under her breath 'I can't believe I'm missing my favourite programme to watch a teacher fiddle about with sticks' – but eventually a thin blue ribbon of smoke rose up out of the wood. Everyone agreed that it was a truly magical sight, to see fire appear out of nowhere like that, and when Mr Swann buried the lit cloth in a nest of straw and the fire began to glow more fiercely, there was a spontaneous burst of applause. It was just beginning to get dark and the evening wind was rustling the new leaves. An unseen owl hooted and Cassie felt again with a thrill that sense of hidden mystery which being in the woods always gave her. Looking around at the group of girls, some eager, others unimpressed, she knew that only a few of those who had turned up to the first session would stay on, but it would be better that way. There would be just a small group of them who were all into exploring nature and having adventures.

As they were walking back to school, Bella said,

'Poor Mr Swann. Did you notice how sad he looked?'

'Not particularly,' replied Abigail.

'He did. You could see in his eyes that he was heartbroken.'

'OK, if you say so. Anyway,' said Abigail, changing the subject instantly, 'are you coming to the premiere party or not?'

Bella looked distraught, 'Well, obviously I can't think of anything I'd more like to do, but the thing is I'm supposed to be going to a music festival with Megan's family at half-term.'

'So cancel,' said Abigail with a shrug. 'Say something else came up.'

'Look, I'll talk to Megan about it, OK? I'll see what she thinks.'

*   *   *

From the moment she had first seen her on stage in assembly, Bella was determined to play some kind of trick on Miss Spitzer. She looked as if she took herself too seriously and Bella saw it as her duty to make her lighten up.

'I've got an idea,' said Abigail, as they were hanging out in her room after the first Wilderness Club. 'Why don't you dress up as a boy for the first lesson? It would be so funny. She'll be all confused and wonder how a boy has somehow sneaked into an all-girls school.'

'Great idea,' said Bella. 'And I've just remembered – didn't Flo say her mum had packed her brother's uniform?'

When Bella walked into the drama studio the next day dressed in Flo's brother's school uniform, Miss Spitzer was standing in the middle of the floor with a fixed smile on her face. But as soon as she saw Bella the smile melted off her cheeks like sweaty face-paint. She wrinkled her tight forehead and said in a traffic cop voice: 'Excuse me, miz, what is your name and what are you wearing?'

Bella started in surprise and replied innocently, 'My name's Ben, Miss Spitzer.' Then she looked down at her own clothes and around at everyone else. 'Oh no, is this a girls' school? Great! Nobody told me. I feel really stupid now! Looks like I'm the only boy here.'

Miss Spitzer gave Bella a look of extreme irritation and grabbed hold of her sleeve, 'Come with me please, young lady.'

Bella saw that it wasn't going well and backed down instantly.

'OK, OK, sorry,' she said, holding up her hands. 'I'm really Bella. I was just dressing up like a boy for fun. Like they do in *As You Like It*!' she grinned hopefully. 'Sorry, it was just a little joke.'

Miss Spitzer didn't find it remotely amusing. She was still pinching Bella's sleeve and looking like she wanted to pinch more than her sleeve, but she let go of it eventually and said in an icy voice, 'Go change. There's no need for you to come back to this session. Perhaps we can make a new start tomorrow.'

'But I'm Rosalind in the play,' pleaded Bella.

'So I see,' said Miss Spitzer, consulting her cast list. 'That's unfortunate, but nevertheless we won't be needing you today, thank you very much, young lady.' She was trying to sound calm and controlled but her voice was shaking with anger. She pointed towards the door and Bella left the room.

Miss Spitzer's unamused reaction to Bella's trick set the tone for what was to come. She had told them, '*You can call me Spitzy if you like – as my nickname*', but nobody did. When they addressed her as Miss Spitzer, she actually corrected them and encouraged them to use her self-appointed nickname instead, whilst winking conspiratorially as if it was all a hoot. And yet when it came to drama, she was brutally straight-faced. Far from having 'a whole bunch of fun', they didn't even have a sliver of fun, because Miss Spitzer took the sessions incredibly seriously. For the first few lessons, she took them through a series of exercises which involved them doing silly things like pretending to be slugs meeting each other on a leaf, which was fine, but they weren't allowed to laugh about it, and if anyone did, Miss Spitzer sent them out. She looked deeply hurt every time anyone giggled, whereas with Miss Flanders it had all been about giggling. And the warm-up exercises seemed to take days to get through. It wasn't until the fourth lesson with her that they actually started rehearsing the first Act of the play, and by then everyone was itching to get on with it.

They started with the scene where Rosalind first falls in love with Orlando who has come to the Duke's court for a wrestling match. Zoe, who was playing Orlando, was tall and muscular, and when the love-struck Rosalind said to her, '*You have wrestled well, and overthrown more than your enemies*', Zoe pretended to be a sumo wrestler: she beat her chest, picked Bella up and threw her down on the floor. It didn't hurt and they all had a good laugh, but Miss Spitzer didn't get the joke at all. She frowned and shouted, 'Zowie! Waddaya think you're doing? You could rilly have hurt Bella. That's not a very matoor way to behave, young lady. Think carefully about the consequences of your actions next time please.'

As for the idea of doing the play in the woods, she thought the girls were joking when they suggested it, and when she realised they weren't, she gave them a long lecture about how dangerous it would be.

'It's not only the issue of the cold, there's also the safety of the audience to consider. Who knows when a branch might fall from a tree? Not to mention the bacteria from the dirt on the forest floor and general lack of hygiene out there.'

All in all, the drama girls were agreed that they had never had so little fun in their whole lives. After the first rehearsal, Bella plucked up the courage to talk to Abigail about the premiere party.

'Listen Abi, I've been thinking about the premiere party and as much as I would love to go, I can't let Megan down like that. She asked me to go to the festival ages ago and I can't just dump her. Sorry. I'm sure someone else really lucky would love to go.'

Abigail flicked her a sideways look and shrugged, 'Fine, suit yourself. Your loss.'

And she walked off. Bella felt as if she'd had a bucket of freezing water tipped over her.

Chapter 7: *It all goes wrong*

It was a rainy Tuesday afternoon, and Megan and Flo were marching down the corridors with their arms linked, cheerfully humming different tunes, Megan with her violin slung over her shoulder and Flo swinging her flute. Despite the grey day, they were looking forward to their first music rehearsal for *As You Like It*. Both were singing and playing in the production and each had a solo, Megan *Under the Greenwood Tree* and Flo *Blow, Blow, Thou Winter Wind*, which meant that they got to take small parts in the play. In a term whose highlight would otherwise have been the Spring Concert, this provided some welcome excitement. As they walked along, their humming got louder and louder as they tried to drown each other out, until eventually they burst into Mr Swann's music room singing their different songs at the tops of their voices. Flo immediately tripped over the strap of Mr Swann's bag, scattering sheets of music all over the floor, and they collapsed laughing.

'Would you mind quietening down a bit,' said Mr Swann politely from the other side of the room, 'I've got some day-old chicks in here. They've only just hatched. Come and see.'

'You keep baby chicks?' cooed Megan. 'How cute!'

'Oh no!' groaned Flo.

They both looked at her in surprise, and then Megan realised and said, 'Oh I get it, your mum. I forgot.' She explained to Mr Swann, 'Her mum rescues old chickens from battery cages. She's kind of had enough of them at home.'

But even Flo couldn't resist the scrawny, damp chicks which were tottering unsteadily around the cage.

'They're adorable! How come you've got them?'

'I got them from a local farm,' explained Mr Swann. 'I felt I needed some company. It can get a bit lonely in here.'

Megan and Flo exchanged significant looks.

'Especially now that –' began Flo, and then stopped.

'Now that what?' asked Mr Swann.

'Now that Spring is here,' said Megan hastily to cover up for Flo.

'Yes quite,' said Mr Swann doubtfully. 'Anyway, we'll start with *Under the Greenwood Tree*. It's a celebration of the simplicity of nature, compared with the complexity of the world that humans create.'

They practised the songs for an hour and then looked at their parts for the instrumental ensemble.

It was the end of the afternoon and the session was just about to end when Cassie burst into the room breathless.

'Hi you two. Mr Swann, I've had an idea. I think we need a theme tune for Wilderness Club. You know, a song we can sing around the campfire at every session.'

'Splendid idea,' said Mr Swann, 'what about this one?' and he got Megan and Flo to sing *Under the Greenwood Tree*.

'Um, not quite what I had in mind,' said Cassie as tactfully as possible. 'I was thinking of something a bit more, you know, modern?'

'Thanks!' said Flo

'Sorry, nothing against you two –I'm sure it sounded really cool back in the olden days – but you know, I want something a bit more up-to-date.'

'Well, why not get someone to compose a new version of it,' suggested Mr Swann. 'You could change the words a bit to make it more suitable.'

'How about Daisy?' said Megan.

So Cassie, Flo and Megan left Mr Swann in his music room and went off to find Daisy.

In Fonteyn, Bella was sitting on her bed feeling miserable. The rain was lashing against the windows, and although she had loads of work to do, all she could seem to do was flick idly through the pages of a magazine that she wasn't even looking at. The afternoon drama session had been a flop. She and Abigail had been rehearsing the scene where Rosalind is thrown out by her uncle and Celia decides to run away with her. Whilst they were acting, Abigail was fine – she hugged Bella close as if they were the best of friends, and laid her head on her shoulder as if she never wanted to be parted from her. In fact, she acted so well and was so convincing and so moving in the role of Celia that Miss Spitzer was falling over herself to praise her. But as soon as there was a break in rehearsals, Abigail refused to speak to Bella, or even look at her. At afternoon break, not realising that everything had completely changed, Bella had said to Abigail, 'Hey, this week's issue of *Movie Maniac* has a really cool centre spread of Jed Brogan.'

'So? What are you telling me for?' Abigail shrugged, before linking arms with Lauren and walking off. Lauren was delighted to have her twin back and smiled back over her shoulder at Bella, who was standing on her own in the middle of the room feeling completely stupid.

The rest of the afternoon session had gone from bad to worse. Bella's acting was flat and distracted. She found she couldn't concentrate on being Rosalind, and she kept forgetting her lines, so that Miss Spitzer, who clearly didn't like her anyway, was constantly poking her with means comments: 'Come on, Bella! Say it like you mean it. You sound like a robot.'

'Oh, for goodness sake! We've been over this bit a hundred times. How long will it take you to get it?'

This was made even more annoying by the fact that Bella was normally brilliant at learning lines. But the fakeness of having to pretend to be best buddies with Abigail was too uncomfortable and she couldn't get into it.

'Come on,' she kept telling herself, 'it's *acting* for goodness' sake. You're meant to *act*. It's *meant* to be fake!' But it was no use.

When Cassie came back into Fonteyn to get her books for prep, Bella was still lying on her bed staring up at the ceiling.

'Hey, what's up? Haven't you got prep to do?'

'Yeah, but I can't concentrate,' sighed Bella.

'You're not still feeling bad about Miss Flanders are you?'

'Well I wasn't, but now that you mention it, there's that too,' she said miserably. 'And Abigail is completely ignoring me because I said I couldn't go to the premiere party with her. Which obviously I would love to go to anyway.'

Cassie went over and sat on her bed.

'Sorry to say it, but I knew Abigail would be like that. She kind of picks people up and drops them.'

'Yeah, I realise that now. But meanwhile, we've got to act together every day. It's excruciating. Anyway,' she suddenly sat up and swung her legs round on to the floor, 'I've got to get over it and get on with it. I know, I think I'll write to Miss Flanders. Apparently she's in Scotland staying at her mother's and I can get the address from the office. I really miss her, you know.'

*   *   *

In the next drama session, Miss Spitzer decided to try out Bella's understudy Willow in the part of Rosalind. Everyone always said what a sensitive actress Willow was, and how she had such emotional depth, but she was also delicate and easily hurt. Miss Spitzer sidled up to her smiling, 'Wee-low. That's such a pretty name. Is it traditional Asian Indian?'

'No, it's a tree.'

'Oh yes, you're right, the willow tree, of course. I thought maybe it was traditional to your culture.'

'Well, I'm really called Priya but my parents always called me Willow because I was always crying – you know, weeping willow – and it kind of stuck.'

'I see.'

Miss Spitzer found it difficult to keep her smiles going for very long and it was clear from her bored face that she wanted Willow to talk less.

'Well anyway, I think it's important for understudies to have plenty of rehearsal time, just in case they have to step up, so maybe you'd like to play Rosalind today.'

'Well, not really because I've got a bad cold and I just heard yesterday that my cat's ill so I'm feeling a bit funny.'

Miss Spitzer's voice was thin with impatience, 'Willow, I wasn't asking you if you'd like to, I was telling you that you will be playing Rosalind today.'

'Oh sorry, I thought you asked me if I'd like to.'

'Enough!' spat Miss Spitzer.

Willow jumped. She wasn't meaning to be rude, she had genuinely misunderstood. She fumbled under her chair for her copy of the play and folded it over at the right page, all the time staring hard at the page and trying to control herself.

They started the scene where Celia teases Rosalind, saying she knows who wrote the poems on the trees because she's seen him, but refusing to tell her who it is. But Abigail made it so difficult for Willow that she seemed to lose her ability to act. Every time she stumbled on a line, or said something in the wrong sort of way, Abigail put her hands on her hips and raised her eyes, and eventually Willow ended up in tears and Bella had to take her part back. A few moments later, Miss Spitzer got a message through on her mobile. She rapped her knuckles loudly against the wall to stop them.

'I have to make an important call to New York,' she explained. 'You can all get on with learning your lines while I'm away,' and she dashed out, letting the door bang behind her.

The room was dull and heavy. No one could get into the play and no one felt like learning lines. Everyone seemed to be feeling low, so Bella decided it was time to cheer things up a bit. As soon as Miss Spitzer had left the room, she jumped up, took centre stage and began imitating her, strutting around the room with her hands on her hips, sticking her backside out and giving the occasional wiggle. When anyone laughed, she would turn on them and wag her finger, 'Now, do you think that's very matoor behaviour, young lady? Uh-uh, I don't think so.'

In all the commotion and hoots of laughter, nobody noticed Abigail slip away, but minutes later the room went suddenly quiet as one by one the girls caught sight of the athletic figure of Miss Spitzer framed in the doorway. She had come back unexpectedly early and caught the end of Bella's performance. There was no mistaking the strong American accent and the habit Miss Spitzer had of tucking her hair firmly behind her ears over and over again at frantic speed, which Bella now imitated perfectly. Even Bella, not one to get easily embarrassed, had the decency to blush when she realised Miss Spitzer was standing behind her.

The awkward silence lasted for what seemed like ages until it was broken by Miss Spitzer's quietly furious voice, 'Bella Santini, please leave the room.'

As Bella walked past her, she added.

'Go straight to Mrs Frost's office. I will meet you outside her door after this lesson.'

As soon as Bella had left the room, Miss Spitzer looked around at the group of girls with strong distaste and said in a wounded voice, 'It's lucky Abigail happened to call me back about poor Willow's eye, or I might not have found out how you all really feel about me. Where is Willow by the way?'

'Oh, her eye's OK now, Miss Spitzer,' said Abigail hurriedly, looking very awkward.

Everyone looked at Willow, who shrugged her shoulders and said, 'There's nothing wrong with my eye.'

'Well you told *me* there was,' hissed Abigail, 'I was really worried.'

The feeling in the room was now worse than ever. A cold hush filled the whole space and no one could bring themselves to look at Abigail. But she seemed oblivious to this, and suggested brightly to Miss Spitzer, 'Hey, I've got an idea Miss Spitzer. Maybe I could be Rosalind for this rehearsal. I know the part really well. And that would give Lauren a chance to step up as Celia. We've done some work on it together and she's really good. I mean I don't mind either way, but I think it would be really nice to give Lauren a chance. She's worked so hard.'

Miss Spitzer, pleased to have an ally in the room, seemed happy to let Abigail take charge.

'OK, Abigail. Look girls, this session's gotten off to a rilly bad start but I like to remember that things can always change for the better. Maybe we can all think about the consequences of our actions while I'm away' – she was one of those people who said 'we' and 'our' when they meant 'you' and 'your' – 'because the way you've all behaved has rilly hurt my feelings. You're smart girls and I know you can rilly give this some sirious thought.'

It was so awkward hearing a teacher talk about her feelings in this obvious way that the girls kept their eyes firmly on the ground, and Miss Spitzer seemed pleased with their apparent show of humility.

'Good. Now I still have to make that call, so when I get back we'll start the rehearsal over and we'll do what you suggest Abigail. I'm not sure Willow feels up to taking on the role of Rosalind today.'

And from that day onwards, without anyone quite knowing how it happened, Abigail became Rosalind and Lauren became Celia.

As Bella explained tearfully to the Fonteyn girls that night in the dorm, Miss Spitzer had demanded that Bella be taken off the production. She had told Mrs Frost that their teacher-pupil relationship was damaged beyond repair and that she could no longer see a way to work with Bella. Mrs Frost was so humiliated by the incident, which shed such an unflattering light on Starlight girls in general, that she had agreed to Miss Spitzer's demands instantly.

'I thought, for some reason, that she would be on my side,' sobbed Bella, 'but far from it. She said I had brought disgrace on the school and what would Miss Spitzer report back about us supposedly well-brought up English girls.'

It was when Mrs Frost used the word 'disgrace' that she had really burst out crying.

'It was so embarrassing,' said Bella, 'you know, not just a silent weep, but big messy blubbery crying that you can't stop.'

They all hugged her at the same time and tried to think of comforting things to say, but really there was nothing comforting that they *could* say. It was just about the worst thing that could happen to any performer. Bella blew her nose loudly.

'Thanks – you – guys,' she hiccupped between sobs. 'But what on earth am I going to do for the rest of the term?'

Chapter 8: *The Woodshed Theatre*

It was Cassie's idea. She wasn't sure when she had first thought about it, but it seemed as if the idea had come to her the very first time she saw the abandoned shed that night in the woods.

'We'll call it the Woodshed Theatre,' she said to her thrilled audience in Fonteyn dorm. Their faces lit up, as if they were already leaning over a campfire. 'It will be the coolest thing ever,' said Bella, staring awestruck into space. 'Just think. Our very own theatre. Our very own production.'

'We could call it *As We Like It*,' said Megan, grinning.

They were all so excited at the thought that they danced around the room.

'*As We Like It*,' said Jasmine dreamily. 'Not as *you* like it, but as *we* like it. I'm going to start writing it straight away.' She pulled out her notebook, wrote *As We Like It* at the top and underlined it twice. Then she looked up, puzzled, 'What *do* we like, anyway?'

'Well, you know, something fun and free and … and … and frivolous.' Cassie waved her arms around vaguely to indicate fun and freedom. Jasmine went back to chewing the end of her pen for a few moments.

'How about: two sisters run away from their strict boarding school where they are training to be nuns and …

and … and join the circus. A travelling circus. They're orphans – so actually it could be an orphanage, training them to be nuns, horribly cruel place. And they join a passing circus, and train to walk the high wire and ride dancing ponies. Then they find out that the circus master is their long-lost father and they all ride off together in a gypsy caravan. The end.'

They all loved the idea. And a moment later, Cassie had an even better one: 'And that song Daisy's writing – the gypsy jazz version of *Under the Greenwood Tree* – it can be our play's theme tune and I'll choreograph a dance for it. Hooray!' she whooped, 'my first jazz dance.'

'Calm down, calm down all of you,' said Bella, her face suddenly dropping. 'Just wait a minute.'

Bella had never uttered the words 'calm down' before in her life, but the experience of being taken off the school production had changed her.

'It's all very well talking about it, but just when exactly are we going to do all of this? And how?'

There was silence for a moment as they began to realise that their fantastic dreams were no more than that – dreams. They would never *really* be able to put on a play in the woods. It was just a lovely idea. They flopped back on their beds gloomily. Then Cassie's voice broke the silence: 'Actually, I've already thought about that,' she said, smiling from ear to ear. 'Wilderness Club – it gives us the perfect opportunity. We'll have to fool Mr Swann into helping us without knowing it, but I've got a feeling that won't be too hard. We can rehearse during Monday night sessions. I mean we'll do a quick bit of bushcrafty stuff first, then get on with it. And we can use our week-end out in the woods to fix up the Woodshed Theatre, and make props and things.'

One by one, the smiles made their way back on to the girls' faces. It seemed like it might just be possible.

'We'll have to keep the play short,' said Megan, re-suming her role as the sensible one again. 'There's no point being over-ambitious. Just three scenes – the girls in the strict orphanage being treated cruelly, then run-ning away and joining the travelling circus in the woods, then the revelation that the circus master is their father.'

'Megan and me will have to pull out of the music in the school production,' said Flo. 'I'll tell Mr Swann – if Bella goes, we go.'

She smiled shyly, pleased with the phrase. She had never said anything so rebellious in her life.

'And I've just had another thought,' Flo turned to Cassie, 'isn't your friend Milo a brilliant gymnast? Maybe he could be in it somehow – as one of the circus acrobats – and my brother Tom is really good at jug-gling. He did a circus skills workshop last summer, you know, just in case he ever had to run away and fend for himself. *And* he could play his trumpet in the jazz song – he's really good at that too.' She clapped her hands in excitement.

They talked frantically about how it all might work and then got straight down to the business of allocating parts: Bella and Cassie would play the two orphaned sisters,

Megan would be the horrible orphanage mistress, with the others filling in as spare orphans. Flo would be the circus master turned long-lost father and would also play her flute, whilst Milo and Tom would stand in as acrobats and musicians.

'If we really want this to work,' said Cassie, 'we're going to have to let my dad in on the secret too. That way, we can all rehearse at my house over half term and then he can organise Milo coming down for the performance.'

'And Tom's school always breaks up before ours,' said Flo, 'so I'm sure we can get him to come down for the performance too.'

'It might just work,' said Bella, her eyes sparkling again, 'I think it really might just work.'

None of them could get to sleep that night. They were all talked out by the time the lights were switched off by Miss Mackenzie, but they lay there silently, their eyelids fluttering and their minds racing with the thrill of it all. How amazing – to put on their own play in the woods!

*   *   *

In the very next session of Wilderness Club, they set to work fixing up the old woodshed. Cassie had roped Mr Swann in to help, on the pretext that the woodshed would act as the Wilderness Club headquarters. It was a fairly large shed, which could comfortably have stabled a horse or two, but its wooden-slatted walls were beginning to crumble, the roof was peeling off, and one of the glass panels in the door had broken. There was a rusty padlock hanging loose from the bolt, and inside were the broken deck chairs and the metal stove with its battered kettle and teapot, which Cassie had noticed when she first came across it. Evidently, it had once been the refuge of a former groundsman, but it was clear that it hadn't been used for years. Mr Swann said they would have to replace the roof, so he got hold of a stepladder and began by tearing off the old roof felt and nailing on a temporary tarpaulin. He whistled cheerfully as he climbed up the ladder and looked as if he was thoroughly enjoying himself, ripping off the mouldy felt and letting the old nails pop out all over the place.

Cassie, who had been helping Bella sweep out the shed, came bounding over to the bottom of his ladder.

'Hey, Mr Swann, have you got a saw? I've just thought – we could make some benches out of fallen branches. You know, for the audience to sit on.'

'The *audience*? What audience?' he asked from the top of his ladder.

Cassie could have kicked herself.

'Did I say audience?' she quickly corrected. 'Sorry, I suppose we get a bit stage obsessed at this school! No, I meant for *us* all to sit on, the club members.'

In that first session, they cleared out the shed and washed it from floor to ceiling, until their faces were covered in grimy smears and their noses and ears were full of cobwebs. The woodshed itself would provide the backdrop to the stage, with the doors propped open and the inside back wall supporting the scenery. They decided – conferring in whispers in the shed – that they would string up a thick rope between two trees, a few paces in front of the shed, to hold the stage curtains. Cassie thought they could attach some long sticks to the top inside corner of each curtain, so that they could open and close them easily.

'I'll get my mum to send some red velvet material,' said Bella. 'She makes all our curtains at home and she'd be delighted to think I had taken up sewing. Very surprised, but delighted. I'm sure Miss Mackenzie will let us use her sewing machine and I bet you can do that kind of thing, Megan.'

'But how will we explain it to Mr Swann?' said Megan. 'It's not exactly normal to string up a random curtain in the woods.'

'We won't string up the curtain 'til the day of the performance,' said Bella. 'And we'll say the rope is for hanging our food up high – out of the reach of bears.'

'Bears?'

'Or whatever.'

Meanwhile, Cassie began to carve a sign saying 'Woodshed Theatre'. She decided that she would carve 'Woodshed' first while Mr Swann was about, and then add the 'Theatre' in secret at some later date. She took inspiration for her design from the school sign at the entrance, which had been made to look like an old scroll, and she used old-fashioned sloping letters. It was fairly painful work cutting out the pencilled letters with a chisel and hammer, since the chisel was constantly slipping and cutting into her hand, but it was also immensely satisfying. By the end of the first session, her shoulders were burning and her nicked hands were stinging, but it was all worth it when she sat back to admire the deep splintery crevices and the jagged curves of the W and the first O.

At the next meeting of Wilderness Club, they sanded down the mossy wooden slats, painted on some wood preserver, and then had a long discussion about what colour they should paint their theatre. Cassie wanted purple and green, but Flo was adamant that school colours would be best.

'How about red and yellow,' argued Bella, 'that's *one* school colour and it would at least be circusy.'

But Flo was insistent: 'Look, we have to do everything we can to make it as likely as possible that Mrs Frost will be pleased with our play,' she hissed.

'Your play? What play?' asked Mr Swann, coming into the shed to get his saw.

Their hearts jolted. But Flo came to the rescue: 'I was just telling the others – it won't be all play, it will be a lot of hard work too,' she quickly clarified.

Cassie joined in:

'And she was trying to convince us that it would make Mrs Frost happy if we painted the thea – the thed – in thchool colourth.'

'Right, then, I'll add red and grey paint to the shopping list,' said Mr Swann, and he walked out humming cheerfully.

'Phew, that was clothe,' giggled Bella.

One of Mr Swann's first purchases had been a canister of gas for the rusty stove, so that they could make drinks while they worked. Jasmine was at that moment sitting cross-legged on the leaf-strewn floor with a mug of hot chocolate at her side, too busy scribbling the lines of the play to get involved in any of the discussions about paint colours. But suddenly she looked up from her pad, 'What do you think? Should one of the orphan sisters fall in love with a circus boy? Or shall we just keep love out of it?'

'Keep love *in* it – definitely!' said Bella. 'And bags me be the one who falls in love. Maybe with Cassie's friend Milo or with Flo's brother Tom.'

'Not Tom,' said Flo immediately, 'that would make him refuse to be in the play.'

'OK, Milo then. I know, he could write me love poems with a sparkler in the dark. That would be so romantic.'

'Hmm, we'll see,' said Jasmine doubtfully. 'Then we would have to do the play in the dark – which, actually, might work quite well. It would make it even more magical. I'll think about it.'

Just then, an old cartwheel came rumbling towards them.

'Watch out!' called Cassie as she came running behind it. It fell over just next to Jasmine, who squeaked in fright. 'I found this not far from the woodshed,' explained Cassie, 'and there's another one with it. Isn't it the coolest? And it's given me the perfect idea: I'm going to make us a gypsy caravan using these old cartwheels – you know, for the orphans to run away in.'

'Hey, we can paint it in school colours!' said Flo, and everyone groaned.

*   *   *

On the last day of school before half term, there was a Spring Picnic at Starlight Academy to which all the families were invited. 'Spring Picnic' was a slightly hopeful name for it, since it was still bitterly cold and cloudy, but Mrs Frost was always trying to set up opportunities for the girls to show off their talents, so everyone tried to get into the spirit of the event. There was going to be a brief performance called *Songs and Dances from the Shows*, followed by a traditional pancake race outside for parents. This was basically an opportunity to make mums and dads fall over in the mud whilst tossing pancakes up in the air from their frying pans, and it was to be followed by a picnic in the tent. After a morning of rehearsals, the whole school spent Thursday afternoon preparing for the rainy picnic. A tent had been set up on the back lawn and it was the job of Years 7 and 8 to decorate it, so the Fonteyn girls had volunteered to make bunting.

They sat at long trestle tables in the dining hall with Miss Mackenzie's sewing machine, cutting out triangles of patterned fabric and sewing them on to a thick red ribbon. But whenever there weren't any teachers in the room, Bella would heave a pile of velvet out from under her chair, and they would quickly get on with sewing the curtains for the Woodshed Theatre.

Bella was furiously hemming the bottom edge of the curtains (she had never picked up a needle before and was constantly yelping as she pricked her fingers), whilst Cassie and Megan carried on with the bunting and Jasmine sewed on the curtain hoops at the top. Meanwhile, Flo kept them entertained with one of her endless family sagas: 'So Tom won two tickets to some Rugby final or other and said he would take Gus – even though Gus is an idiot – you know, you two, you've met him haven't you?' she nodded towards Cassie and Jasmine who heartily agreed, 'but anyway, he decided he would take him because he is his brother after all, and he loves rugby more than anything. Anyway, then Gus got Tom to give him the tickets by saying "let me see them" or something, and now he won't give them back and he's invited a friend from school instead, and Tom doesn't know where he's hidden the tickets so there's nothing he can do about it. And that's why he's got to come to our Spring Picnic with Mum. I talked to him last night and I've never known him so furious.'

They had banned Flo from touching any scissors because she had already slashed a hole in Bella's sleeve and cut a chunk of her own hair off, so she was trying instead to untangle a long string of dragonfly fairy lights, but was actually making them more tangled.

'I love dragonflies,' she mused to herself, 'you'd think they'd be scary, but actually they're really cute.'

At that moment, Miss Spitzer came in and Bella stuffed

the velvet curtains back under her chair. Miss Spitzer pretended to be interested in what everyone was doing: she went round to each group and leant over their work, making fake-sounding encouraging comments, as if she was reading them out of a teaching manual on how to make positive comments.

'Neat sewing, Candy, that's awesome. I *like* what you've done with that napkin, Charlotte, it's super-cute.'

When she came to the table where the Fonteyn girls were working, she clapped her hands like a little girl and said, 'Oooh bunting – how darling! It's so perfectly quaint and English.' Then suddenly her mechanical smile uncranked and she turned to Bella, 'What was that you pushed under the table, Bella?'

There was an agonising silence. They all looked purposefully at the floor. Megan coughed and shuffled in her seat, pressing the pedal of the sewing machine so that it went thundering off at a gallop. Flo knocked a tub of pins to the floor; they scattered across the room and she darted down to gather them in. Cassie was just about to come to the rescue with some elaborate lie, when Bella, with a resigned shrug, pulled the velvet curtains up on to the table and looked Miss Spitzer straight in the eye.

'OK, I'm sorry, you caught me. I probably shouldn't be doing this now, because it's part of my punishment. I have to sew new curtains for Mrs Frost's office.'

A deep crevice appeared down Miss Spitzer's forehead, and she looked as if she was about to tell Bella off, but then suddenly she smiled and gave her shoulder a friendly squeeze.

'You're right, you probably shouldn't be doing it now, but I'll pretend I haven't seen anything.' She did a big obvious wink, and then added, 'I think you've already paid the price for your inappropriate behaviour, and I'm sure you've learnt your lesson.'

As she walked away, Bella hissed under her breath, 'Huh! She won't win me over that easily.'

Miss Spitzer had gone over to the table where Abigail and Lauren were tying ribbons round little tubs of daffodils. They tucked a flower behind her ear and she did a hoopla dancing-girl spin.

*　　*　　*

The Spring Picnic was in full flow and the parents were getting kitted up in their aprons ready for the pancake race. They lined up to get their frying pans, all of which had ready-made pancakes in them, and headed outside in the rain to the starting line.

'I bet my mum is the first to drop hers,' groaned Flo.

'No, my dad has never held any sort of cooking pan in his life,' said Jasmine. 'He's bound to drop it in fright.'

'Well, as long as mine don't burst into song on the way, I don't mind,' said Bella. 'I'm just relieved they haven't dressed up in their traditional old-English costumes and brought their maypole.'

The race involved lots of shrieking and laughter, which was all their parents ever seemed to do when they came to Starlight Academy – it was no wonder they were always going on about how school days were the best days of your life. At the end, they were all suitably covered in mud and none of them had managed to keep their pancakes in the frying pan, except for Cassie's dad, who had calmly and carefully flipped his pancake whilst walking all the way at a leisurely pace.

'Typical,' said Cassie, 'he never gets carried away.'

But she ran up to give him a hug as he received his prize bottle of champagne, smiling modestly and nodding graciously in recognition of the applause.

For the picnic, Cassie sat with her dad on a rug by the entrance. A draught was making the tent flap open and sending gusts of rain in on them. She could see Flo sitting with her mum and Tom not far away, and she wished they were sitting with them, but she couldn't bring herself to just get up and walk over there. She looked at the dry, thick sandwiches and the wedge of creamy cake on her plate, and she didn't feel like eating any of it.

'So, run this by me again,' her dad was saying, 'your friend Bella was thrown off the school play – for no good reason, of course – and you came up with the idea of putting on your own rival play.'

'Yup,' Cassie nodded absent-mindedly, her thoughts elsewhere.

'In the woods.'

'Yup.'

'In a shed.'

'Yup. That's why it's the Woodshed Theatre.'

'I gathered that. But when do you rehearse? And what's the play? And who's going to watch it? And what on earth will Mrs Frost think?'

Cassie wasn't in the mood to talk about it.

'Look Dad, chill out and stop going on about it.'

He laughed, 'One last thing, if I may, just to get this straight: we're also setting up a rehearsal studio in our house over half-term, and then I'm smuggling two boys into your all-girls school?'

'Yup.'

'Just checking.'

Cassie kissed him on the cheek as she got up, shaking out her stiff legs.

'Thanks, Dad. I'm glad you're like you are.'

The rain had stopped and the sun seemed to be peering half-heartedly through the tent flaps. Cassie was just about to make her way over to Flo when she saw that Flo was walking towards her with Tom in tow.

'I've told Tom about the play,' she whispered, 'and he's interested.'

Tom certainly didn't *look* very interested. He had his hands in his pockets and he was looking expectantly up at the roof of the tent, as if a helicopter might swoop down at any moment and rescue him from this girlish hell.

'Hi,' said Cassie.

'I can't believe I'm at my kid sister's school picnic,' he grumbled to no one in particular. 'I should be at the Six Nations final.'

'So, do you want to come and see the Woodshed Theatre?' Cassie asked.

'OK,' Tom shrugged.

'What are you lot plotting now?' asked Cassie's dad.

'Nothing,' said Cassie. 'Look, I think Flo's mum wants to talk to you.'

She pointed in the direction of Flo's mum, who did look like she wanted to talk to someone, but then she usually looked like that. 'See you later,' and they darted out of the tent.

'Mum's taken it too far this time,' said Flo, shaking her head as they walked away from the tent. 'Did you see? She's actually got chicken poo on her shoulder.'

'I know, I told her in the car,' laughed Tom, 'but she insisted it was toothpaste – as if that was somehow better.'

He seemed to cheer up once they had got outside the tent. They headed towards the woods and just as they reached the gap in the trees it started to rain again.

'I'm going back to get my mac,' said Flo. 'I'll catch you up.'

Inside the woods it was like being inside a house with the rain battering on the roof.

'Hey, try this,' said Tom, 'it's really cool.' And he lay down flat on his back on the ground. Cassie lay down too and waited.

'You have to keep your eyes open and look straight up at the raindrops,' he explained.

Cassie looked up at the sky. The raindrops flew down at an immense speed, getting alarmingly huge just as they hit your face.

'It *is* really cool,' she said. 'It's like being torpedoed by raindrop dive bombers.'

He laughed.

'That doesn't actually make sense but I know what you mean.'

They got up again after a bit and Cassie reached round to pick something tickly off her neck.

'Hey, a centipede,' she said, and bent her head to watch it crawl across her hand, 'hello little guy.'

Tom frowned curiously, 'You mean you're not frightened of them?'

'Frightened of centipedes?' laughed Cassie. 'Er, no, not really. Giant mutant killer ones maybe, but not ordinary ones.'

Cassie was letting the centipede walk from hand to hand.

'Here,' she said and held out her hand. Tom reached over and she let it walk onto his.

Then Flo appeared, wearing her mac with the hood tightly buttoned up, and carrying an umbrella.

'This is for you two,' she said, holding it out.

They walked on to the Woodshed Theatre and Tom seemed to slump back into his not-at-the-rugby-match gloom.

'I just can't believe it happened,' he moaned. 'It's been such a rubbish term anyway, and that was the only good point in the whole year.'

'Why has it been rubbish?' asked Cassie.

'Oh, work and exams and stuff. You know, subject choices and it's getting all serious and there's hardly any time for sport.'

'What he means is that one cricket practice was can-celled for a GCSE options meeting,' explained Flo.

'I just wish sometimes that I could buy a motorbike and ride away and never come back.'

'Yeah, right!' said Flo, rolling her eyes at Cassie.

It was dark by the time everyone gathered at the front of the school to say goodbye and go home. Whilst their parents packed cars, the girls zipped about looking for their friends in a panic, and calling out urgently if they couldn't find each other. Mr Burrows the caretaker had lit the two Olympics-style torches which flanked the front entrance of the school, and by the light of their flickering flames, they talked and laughed and hugged as if they were parting for a year rather than a week. The Fonteyn girls, plus Flo and Tom, were all standing in a secret huddle, making hushed arrangements for their half-term rehearsals at Cassie's house, when Abigail and Lauren sauntered over.

'Hey Jasmine, do you want my old Converse?' Abigail asked, swinging her gold trainers by the laces. 'Well, ac-tually, they're pretty much new. I've just got some newer ones, that's all.'

'Great, thanks,' said Jasmine. 'That's really kind of you.'

'You should come over to Lauren's some time in half term,' Abigail continued. 'We're having a makeover party.'

Then she suddenly noticed Tom, who was staring hard

into the torch flames, wishing they would consume him.

'Oh, hi, you're Flo's brother. I heard about the Rugby ticket thing. That's so harsh.'

Tom flicked his eyes over in her direction briefly, then looked back at the flames, but Abigail carried on just as boldly, 'I've got a feeling France are going to win the Six Nations anyway,' she said.

They all looked at her in confusion.

'What do *you* know about rugby?' laughed Bella.

Even Lauren giggled and said, 'Yeah, Abi, you hate sport.'

'No I don't,' said Abigail, shooting irritated looks at them all. Then she carried on talking to Tom. 'Hey, I've just had an idea. I've got these tickets for the premiere of *Wild Thing*. My dad's a director and he got them – you know, limo and everything and you get to meet Jed Brogan.'

'Wow, I think he's great,' said Tom, his face lighting up, 'I've seen all his films.'

'Well, you know, you could come with me if you like. If you've got nothing better to do over half-term.'

'Wow, that would be really cool,' said Tom. And then, remembering, he turned to Cassie, 'Which days are we doing that thing at yours again?'

There was an awkward silence and Flo stared hard at Tom, who said, 'Oh yeah, sorry. We're not, are we.'

Abigail scribbled her mobile number on a scrap of paper and handed it to Tom.

'Well look, if you want to go, call me and I'll meet you near Leicester Square.'

Car horns started to hoot and the girls gave each other one last hug and broke away.

'See you in a couple of days,' the Fonteyn girls whispered to each other, 'can't wait!'

Chapter 9: *More Trouble*

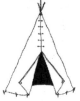

It was Sunday night. Half-term was over and the girls had come back to school that afternoon in a flurry of excitement. Flo was in Fonteyn, sitting on the end of Cassie's bed. She had fifteen minutes to get back to her own dorm before lights-out and they had so much to talk about that a torrent of chatter was tumbling river-like through the room. They had met up at Cassie's house on the Monday of half-term to rehearse their play. Cassie's old school friend Milo had been given the role of circus acrobat, and Tom had played his trumpet and practised his juggling act as the clown. But that now seemed ages ago and they wanted to make more plans for the Woodshed Theatre production of *As We Like It*.

'Oh I forgot to even tell you all,' gabbled Flo, whacking the end of Cassie's bed to get their attention, 'Tom went to the premiere of *Wild Thing* with Abigail.'

'Oh yeah! I'd forgotten all about that,' Bella cut in. 'So how was it?'

'Well, he didn't meet her dad, but he said he must be really important because they went in a limo and were taken to meet Jed Brogan and everything after the film.'

'Wow, to think that could have been me!' said Bella, looking wistful for a moment. Then she shook herself out of it, 'But anyway, we had a brilliant time at the festival, didn't we, Megan? Actually, I don't know why I'm asking *you*.' She whispered loudly behind her hand to the others, 'Megan just sat in the tent reading most of the time.'

'Well, the music was too loud,' said Megan defensively. 'And I can't stand that kind of music anyway.'

'So anyway, I had a great time with Megan's parents,' said Bella. 'But listen, how are we going to get Milo and Tom here for the performance? It's the one big issue we haven't quite sorted out yet.'

'It's OK,' said Cassie. 'I've thought it all through. The school performance of *As You Like It* is on a Saturday night in a few weeks, right? So I'm going to ask Mrs Frost if while the parents are here for the play we can do a demonstration of our bushcraft skills to them. So we'll lead the whole school into the woods and – ta da! – do our play.'

'Brilliant!' said Jasmin.

'My dad can bring Milo to the school play and Flo's mum can bring Tom, and at the interval they can rush down to the woodshed to set it all up and get changed. And Dad has helped me design the gypsy caravan – I'm going to make a cylinder out of bent willow twigs, which we can cover with painted material, and then we can attach that to the wheel-base. He said he drew the line at smuggling a horse into school though, so no horse for the caravan unfortunately. Milo and Tom will just have to pull it.'

There was the beep of a text coming through and Flo urgently grabbed her phone off the bed as if it was about to fly out of the window. As she read it, she blushed and bit her lip.

'Go on then,' smiled Cassie, 'tell us who it's from. You're obviously dying to.'

'No I'm not,' Flo protested, trying hard not to grin. 'It's no big deal, it's just from Milo.' Then she couldn't help adding, 'It's the third time he's texted.'

'What about?'

'Oh, just saying he's found a costume to wear and he'll see us at the play.'

'He'll see *all* of us at the play or he'll see *you* at the play?' quizzed Cassie.

'Well, that's the thing, I can't tell, can I? Because it just says "u", which could mean all of us or just me. It's so annoying.'

There was a sharp rap at the door, 'Flo,' said the warning voice of Miss MacKenzie the housemistress. 'I'm just letting you know that I'm on my way to Hepburn.'

Flo leapt off the bed and rushed for the door.

*   *   *

The first couple of weeks back were packed with intensive classes. The drama girls had their production to prepare for, which most of the music girls were involved in too, and the dancers had just been told of a surprise visit from Greta Liesel, the former prima ballerina. Miss Liesel was a close friend of the daughter of the school's founder Lady Anthea Price, and the dancers would be putting on a performance for her on Founders Day. In addition to all of this, the school work was piling up as they prepared for end of term exams, and one way or another the girls found that they had very little time to rehearse their secret play. For Cassie, Wilderness Club provided the only respite from a punishing schedule of academic and stage work, and when she wasn't working on the woodshed, she was busy choreographing her jazz dance. Daisy had finished her version of *Under the Greenwood Tree*, and had made a recording of it with flute, guitar, trumpet and double-bass backing, so Cassie was completely absorbed in making up a dance routine to go with the music. It was all she could think about, day and night – her dance – and she spent every break-time in the studio trying out new sequences.

One wet Tuesday, when a teacher's absence had prompted an early break, Cassie seized the unexpected opportunity and dashed off to the dance studio to practise her routine. She wanted to get it just right before teaching it to the others, and it wasn't quite there yet. There was no time to change, so she just rolled up her sleeves and hitched up her skirt, before turning up the volume and losing herself in the twanging rhythms of Daisy's music. She flew back and forth across the studio, sliding on its beautifully polished floor as if on ice, loving the freedom of being on her own with the music as it took over her body. She was hot and out of breath – but sure that she had got it at last – when she first thought to look up at the clock. *Damn – she was late! History would have started by now*. Cassie quickly cut the music, stuffed her shirt back into her skirt, tugged at her sleeves, and tried to flatten her hair as she ran back to the classroom at top speed.

Just as she'd thought, the lesson had already started. *Best not to draw attention to myself,* she thought, and tried to slip into the empty seat behind her desk as unobtrusively as possible. But she seemed suddenly to have turned into Flo, and found that she was knocking books off desks, tripping over chair legs and generally announcing her lateness in the most obvious way. Mr Lockwood sighed with a sense of deep suffering and stopped talking while she got into her seat.

'Come on, come on,' he muttered with a look of thinly stretched patience.

Cassie cast a quick look around the room, trying to remember what it was they were doing in History at the moment – that was it, the Industrial Revolution. She strained her eyes to look at the open exercise books on other people's desks. The Industrial Revolution, and new building materials and possibly – she glanced about – bridge-building? Too late it hit her: they were meant to have drawn a design for a bridge and she had forgotten all about it. Cassie panicked, grabbed a pen from the desk next door, and scribbled a quick bridge in her prep book.

It was the most basic bridge imaginable – the kind a five-year-old might draw – a simple arch with a flat line across the top. And it was agonising when she had to stand up and explain her bridge to the class: they barely bothered to stifle their giggles as she sheepishly held up her drawing.

'And what material is it constructed from?' asked Mr Lockwood, shaking his head in wonder.

'Um, wood?' replied Cassie.

'But the whole point of the Industrial Revolution is that metals such as iron began to replace the more traditional building materials such as wood, thus allowing more scope for elaborate design.'

'Oh, metal then,' she said.

But Mr Lockwood wouldn't leave it at that: he was determined to prolong her agony.

'And what sort of scale is it? I mean what distance could it span and how will it stay rigid?'

By this point, Cassie had already lost every shred of dignity, and she couldn't think of any measurements anyway – she had never really got measurements – so she simply stretched her arms out as wide as they would go.

'About this wide,' she announced.

'So, what exactly was this bridge designed to cross?'

'I dunno,' she shrugged, enjoying it now that she had given up, 'the school moat? To escape from here?'

Straight after History, it was Science, and as they bundled down the corridor towards the labs, Cassie felt a sense of mounting frustration: there just wasn't enough time to do the things you wanted to do. It was one thing after another in an endless succession of work and duties. By the time Flo caught up with her in the corridor, she finally exploded: 'We might as well just call the whole thing off! We'll never have time to rehearse and I've got this dance to teach you all but there's no time to do it and it's going to be completely rubbish so why don't we just forget it!'

'Oh, it'll be fine,' beamed Flo. 'We've got the Wilderness Weekend, remember. That'll give us plenty of time to rehearse. I just need to keep myself in one piece until then, and here comes Science – worst luck.'

Flo rarely got through a science lesson without at least electrocuting herself.

'Let's hope I don't set my hair on fire again,' she whispered, 'or we'll be having a bald circus-master in our play.'

Mr Gutenberg the Science teacher loved explosions and took any opportunity to blow things up. He was also nearly as accident-prone as Flo, so they assumed that his lack of hair on the front half of his head was due to similar incidents with fire. Today was to be no exception. Mr Gutenberg burst into the lab with a gleeful grin, 'We're going to make rockets!' he announced.

He filled a glass of water and dropped a big white tablet into it, which fizzed madly and then disappeared.

'That's called an alka-seltzer,' he said. 'You might notice your parents having one after a big party. Gets rid of headaches – in fact, come to think of it –' and he drank the whole glassful in one gulp, before refilling it and dropping in another white tablet. 'Now, when it fizzes like that, it releases a gas. And when that gas is released into a small space with nowhere to go, the pressure builds up and it forces its way out suddenly. In other words it explodes. *But how does that make a rocket shoot up into the sky?* you might ask.'

He waited for a while with an expectant look on his face until Zoe obligingly put up her hand.

'Yes, Zoe?'

'How does that make a rocket shoot up into the sky?'

'Yes, I thought you might ask that. Well, I'll tell you how. Newton's third law of motion. Sir Issac Newton, brilliant scientist and mathematician, worked out that every action has an equal and opposite reaction. *But what does that mean?* you might ask.'

This time, Abigail obliged, 'Yes, Abigail?'

'What does that mean?'

'What does what mean?'

'That thing you said.'

'You might well ask.'

'I did ask.'

'Aha!'

Mr Gutenberg rummaged under his desk and brought out two pairs of roller boots, the old-fashioned lace-up kind.

'Abigail, perhaps you would oblige?' he held up one of the pairs of roller boots and Abigail went up and put them on.

'Now, who will partner Abigail?'

Mr Gutenberg held up the other pair of roller-boots and looked around the room. No one moved or said anything. Lauren – her only potential ally – had a tummy bug. Finally Mr Gutenberg said, 'Florence.'

'Oh, not me, Mr Gutenberg, I have no sense of balance whatsoever. I'll fall over the minute I touch them.'

'Alright. Willow then.'

Tears sprung into Willow's eyes almost immediately.

'Sorry Mr Gutenberg, but Abigail doesn't like me. Please don't make me.'

Abigail was looking more and more annoyed, standing there on her own at the front in her roller-boots.

'Alright, alright. Goodness me, this is supposed to be fun! Cassandra then.'

'No way.' Cassie shook her head firmly.

Mr Gutenberg banged the roller boots down on the lab bench.

'Now, look! I've had just about enough of this. Cassandra, you will come to the front and put the roller boots on this minute.'

Cassie shook her head again.

'Sorry, but I can't. I twisted my ankle over half-term and I'm not allowed to take the risk – you know with my dancing and all that.'

Mr Gutenberg sat down heavily as one of the boots rolled off down the bench and crashed to the floor. He grabbed hold of his side wisps of hair and pulled.

'Will *someone* – please – partner – Abigail?'

Again, there was silence as they all looked hard at their desks.

'But I will, if no one else will,' said Jasmine finally in

a quiet voice, and she went up to the front to put on the roller-boots.

Mr Gutenberg made her and Abigail stand facing each other with the palms of their hands touching.

'Now, push against each others hands.'

They pushed and both rolled backwards.

'You see?' he said, holding up his hands and raising his eyebrows wearily at the class. His demonstration had by now entirely lost its element of fun. 'You push in one direction,' he continued in a bored voice, 'and you get an exactly equal reaction in the opposite direction. They are moving backwards in exactly the same measure as they are pushing forwards. Now, boots off.'

After that, they were put into pairs to make their rockets using a small plastic canister and some coloured card. Abigail had to pair up with Mr Gutenberg because there were odd numbers, and she sat there looking furious as he made a rocket tube, cap and fins out of card to fit around the plastic canister. Finally, they added water to the canister and quickly replaced the lid, then waited whilst it fizzed inside. Within seconds, the lid flew off the plastic canister propelling the rocket up into the air, and they all clapped and cheered, except for Abigail.

It had been such an awful day all round (apart from the precious few minutes spent in the studio) that Cassie was hardly surprised when she was called into Mrs Frost's office at the end of the day. As she walked into the room,

Mrs Frost brushed her with a quick look before turning back to the computer screen and tapping the keyboard with her pearly shell nails for a few more minutes. Cassie sat in silence. Then, suddenly wondering if she was being rude by *not* speaking, she said, 'You wanted to see me.'

Mrs Frost pinned her with a sharp look.

'I know full well that I wanted to see you. I was the one who called you here. Frankly, Cassie, I've had just about enough of your casual insolence. In the staff meeting tonight, Mr Lockwood complained that your attitude in history is slapdash at best, and often downright rude. Mr Gutenberg mentioned that you also refused to co-operate in his lesson –'

'I wasn't the only –'

'I haven't finished!' She stuck another pin in. 'Now, either you will shape up, pay proper attention in class, and speak courteously to your teachers, or you will be put on special measures.'

Out of nowhere, and without her being able to control it, fat tears began to roll one after another down Cassie's cheeks. And before she knew it, her shoulders were heaving with great sobs.

'I don't – mean – to – be – rude,' she choked. 'And I'm trying, I really am. I want to be good. I wish there was some way I could prove to you that I can be.'

Mrs Frost's face softened instantly. She got up from behind her desk and went round to comfort Cassie, laying an arm over her shoulders in a gesture which was meant to be a hug but which was so awkward that it felt more like a thin, ill-fitting scarf.

'I can see that you do, my dear, I can see that you do. And I happen to have an idea. You already know, I believe, that we have a very special visitor coming at the end of the week – Miss Greta Liesel, who will join us for Founders Day. She arrives in the afternoon, and I would like *you* to show her around the school. You're one of our finest dancers and it would give you a chance to show our school in its best light, as well as showing me that you can act responsibly, that you can take a job on and really fulfil it properly.'

Chapter 10: *Founder's Day*

Special trips had been organised for the morning of Founders Day, and Years 7 and 8 were due to go bowling. As they all waited outside the front of school for the coach to arrive, Abigail and Lauren walked over to the where the Fonteyn girls were standing in a line doing each other's hair. Megan was at the back, because she refused to let anyone touch her hair. She was doing French braids in Bella's hair, and Bella was trying to scrape Cassie's hair into two small sticking-out bunches, whilst Cassie tried to rearrange Jasmine's new long fringe.

'Don't wear it to the side like that,' she said, flipping it this way and that. 'It makes you look like ... you know who.'

And just then the synthetic twins themselves walked up. Abigail looked Jasmine up and down, and pointed at the trainers she had given her before half-term.

'Hey Jasmine, I can't believe you're wearing gold Converse. They're so over.'

To everyone's surprise, quiet, sweet Jasmine broke away from the line and stepped up to face Abigail with her hands on her hips: 'Actually Abigail, my parents don't have all that much money so they don't buy me clothes all the time so consequently I'm not necessarily up-to-date with every latest fashion and I have to rely on the so-called kindness of people like *you* to give me their old stuff. But you know what? I don't mind. What my clothes look like is *not* the most important thing about me. And if you think it's the most important thing about *you*, then poor you, because there can't be much else very interesting about you.'

By the end of her speech, her voice was trembling and she promptly burst into tears. The Fonteyn girls gathered round and encircled her in a protective hug.

'Whatever,' said Abigail, linking arms with Lauren and turning to go. 'Luckily we'll all be wearing those gross bowling shoes soon, so you'll probably feel right at home.'

The coach drew up and they all piled on. The bowling and cinema complex was half an hour away, so there was plenty of time on the coach to sort out partners and teams. There was also plenty of time for Lauren to feel sicker and sicker. She was the kind of girl who felt sick just looking at a roundabout or opening a car door, so the long, winding coach journey was unbearable torture. By the time they reached the bowling alley, she had to be rushed off to the toilets by Miss Chivers, whilst the rest of them went to get their shoes and bowling balls. Jasmine was just pulling her shoes on, when Abigail slipped into the seat next to her with a big smile on her face. She gave Jasmine a friendly dig in the ribs.

'Hey, I was only joking about the Converse by the

way. Obviously I love them 'cause I gave them to you, didn't I?'

Jasmine looked blankly at Abigail.

'Oh, OK,' she murmured.

'In fact, I've got some other stuff you can have if you want.'

'It's OK, I don't need anything at the moment, thanks.'

Bella came over to where they were sitting with Antonia, Katie, Willow and Zoe in tow.

'Ready, Jasmine? We're relying on you turning out to be a bowling ace, by the way. It's me, you, Cassie and Willow against Antonia, Katie, Zoe and Flo for goodness' sake! We haven't a hope. I'm rubbish, Cassie's middling, and Willow's never picked up a bowling ball in her life, so it's all down to you.'

'Actually,' laughed Antonia, '*I've* never picked up a bowling ball in my life either.'

'Yeah, well obviously you're going to be a super-star at it like you are at everything else. And Katie will be the same. Our only hope is that Flo will manage to throw her ball backwards and knock you both out. Come on, let's go.'

'Hey, you guys. Can I join your team?' Abigail called out after them. 'Lauren and me were supposed to be with Daisy and Megan, but now that Lauren's not well they've decided to join other teams. So it's just me.'

'Sorry,' said Bella. 'We've worked it all out. It would make the teams unbalanced.'

'But I could help you. I'm pretty good at bowling, you know. Why not put Willow with the teachers if she's rubbish?'

'It's OK, thanks,' said Bella. 'We'd rather just lose. Look, here come Miss Chivers and Miss Hurley. It looks like they need someone on their team.'

So Abigail was forced to choose between sitting out altogether or joining the teachers' team. She decided to sit out and spent the rest of the session looking miserable on a bench with a white-faced Lauren.

'At least we don't have to wear those uncool shoes,' said Lauren weakly.

It turned out that the only bowling ace was Willow. She was delighted about her hidden talent, and couldn't stop whooping for joy and dancing madly every time she bowled another strike.

'You *must* have done this before,' said Antonia suspiciously.

'Never, I swear!' Willow beamed.

Antonia, on the other hand, was completely useless at bowling, and the others couldn't help betraying their glee.

'Sorry,' smiled Bella, clapping her hands as another of Antonia's balls rolled pathetically into the gutter, 'but, at last! Something you're no good at.'

Antonia took it very well and laughed along with the others about how terrible she was.

After a snack break, they juggled teams and started

again. Abigail sidled up to Willow as she was drinking her milkshake and said, 'Hey, Willow, you were brilliant. Let's pair up for the next round.'

'No thanks,' said Willow.

'Look, I'm only trying to be friendly,' returned Abigail. 'I'd have thought that you of all people could use some extra friends.'

And she strode off, muttering about how bowling was a stupid uncool game for stupid uncool people. But Willow was too excited about being a secret bowling star to care about anything else, and she skipped off to join the others for the next round.

On the coach on the way home, Abigail made a beeline for Bella and slid into the seat next to her.

'Hey,' she said with a friendly smile, as if nothing had ever happened between them.

'Hey,' muttered Bella, turning to look out of the window as the coach pulled away and chugged off.

'You know, I was thinking,' Abigail continued in the same breezily cheerful tone, 'I could get you back in the play if you like.'

Bella turned her head sharply.

'You what?'

'I could get you back in the play. I could have a word with Spitzy – she pretty much does whatever I say, and I know I could swing it. If you want me to, I mean. You could be Celia maybe.'

Bella was too amazed and appalled to speak. She just stared at Abigail, open-mouthed.

'But what about Lauren?' she said finally. 'She's Celia.'

Abigail shrugged.

'Up to you – I'm just saying, I could do it if you want.'

Bella could feel a volcano of anger bubbling inside her. Her face flushed red and she tried to contain herself as she hissed, 'No thanks, Abigail. Actually, I'm not sure I'm going to make it to the play anyway – I've got something else on that night. Something much better.'

Abigail was on her in an instant, like a crow swooping down onto a flattened carcass.

'What? What have you got on?'

Bella sensed immediately that she had gone too far and tried to back up. The colour drained from her face as she stammered, 'Oh, nothing. Nothing really. Forget I said it.'

But now Abigail was even more suspicious. Her eyes narrowed, 'Hang on a minute – I *knew* there was something going on. What is it? Come on, you can tell me.'

'It's nothing,' said Bella firmly, crossing her arms and turning to stare out of the window again.

*　　*　　*

When they got back to school, Cassie found that her afternoon ballet class had been cancelled for some reason, so she seized the opportunity to work on the gypsy caravan. She hadn't been able to do much on it since half term, and now would be the perfect opportunity: she could fix the canvas cover around the willow frame and maybe even start painting it. So as soon as lunch had finished, she tore up to the dorm, flung on her jeans and a sweatshirt, and ran all the way down to the Woodshed so that she could get on with it as quickly as possible. Thrilled at the prospect of getting to build her beloved caravan at last, Cassie unlocked the woodshed with a pounding heart and trembling fingers.

She pulled out the bent willow frame and balanced it on the ground, where it rolled and bounced lightly across the dirt floor. Then, unfolding the white canvas sheet she had stored in the shed, she draped it over the frame. She had measured it all up at home and had sewn on some ties to attach the cover to the willow sticks. She would have to hurry if she wanted to start painting it any time soon, but her fingers were fumbling and useless – they felt like overgrown carrots – and it was so awkward fiddling with the little ties and the bendy frame. Ballet had been cancelled, she knew that much, but she was sure Mrs Frost would probably dream up some other 'useful activity' to take up her time if she let her – best to get on with something useful herself. She had just tied the last loop around the last willow hoop, when the recollection suddenly struck her like a dagger in the heart. Greta! Greta Liesel! She was meant to be showing her around the school. *That* was why ballet had been cancelled. She dropped what she was doing immediately, and without even putting the caravan frame away, or locking up the woodshed, she raced back to school as fast as her legs would carry her, stumbling over tree roots all the way.

Back in the dorm, Cassie looked around in a panic like a fugitive on the run. The details had all come back to her on the way back from the woods: she was meant to meet Greta Liesel at two o'clock in Reception and take her on a tour of the school, ending up at the dance studio, where some of the older girls would put on a brief performance at 2.30. She looked at the clock on her bedside table – 2.10 – if *only* she could roll back time! Miss Liesel would be standing there in reception waiting for her at this very minute. She was so out of breath that each painful rasp burnt her throat as she tried hard to calm down and think what on earth she could do. She grabbed her uniform off the bed and the clock clicked onto 2.11. There was no time to take her jeans off. She stepped into her skirt, falling over and scrambling to her feet again as she hopped around the room on one leg. She wrenched off her hoodie and pulled her school jumper over her head, then, as she leapt down the stairs two at a time, desperately tried to push her jeans up her legs under her school skirt.

Greta Liesel was still standing there in Reception, smiling around expectantly. Cassie all but screeched to a halt in front of her, patting down her wild hair and trying to get her breath back. She checked her jeans – they were safely tucked up over her knees – held out her hand, and gave Miss Liesel a huge grin.

'I'm *so* sorry to have kept you waiting, Miss Liesel. I'm Cassie March and I'm going to be showing you round the school.'

The dancer took her hand gently and smiled. She was beautiful, with smooth dark hair pinned back from her ivory face, and sparkling eyes that creased up as she smiled.

'Nice to meet you, Cassie,' she said. Her hand was long and thin and Cassie thought she could feel the delicate bones crushing together as she shook it enthusiastically. Without losing another moment, she led her special guest off through the double doors, chatting all the way about how much she loved being at Starlight Academy and telling her about their performance of *The Nutcracker* the previous term, in which she had taken the starring role. She was beginning to think that she might actually have got away with it. Mrs Frost didn't seem to be about, so she might never even find out that Miss Liesel had been kept waiting. It seemed that disaster – for once – had been averted.

They had been around all the classrooms, and the theatre, and some of the music rooms and were just on their way to the dance studio, when Cassie felt one leg of her jeans slipping down over her knee. She tried to reach down and subtly tug it up, but Miss Liesel was looking straight at her, telling her about the time *she* had played Clara in *The Nutcracker*. There was nothing she could do about it: gradually, bit by bit, it was inching down her leg, tickling her madly. And then just as they reached the dance studio, it finally dropped all the way to the floor. As soon as one leg had dropped, the other side seemed to let out a sigh of relief and followed it to the floor. Cassie kept on walking, looking straight ahead as they went down the corridor, in the hope that Greta too would only look straight ahead and not down at her jeans. But then, of course, Mrs Frost came into view.

'Ah, *there* you are!' she was saying from the other end of the corridor, her eyebrows raised into severe arches. She was heading towards them. And *she* certainly wasn't looking straight ahead: she was looking down at the lower half of Cassie's legs.

It was like those dreams when you arrived at school and realised you were naked, Cassie thought. And you spent the whole day trying to avoid people and ducking behind tall plants (*why in those dreams didn't you ever just go and put some clothes on?* she wondered). This wasn't quite as bad as that, but it wasn't far off. She could feel Mrs Frost's eyes on her jeans, and her cheeks burnt up, but she didn't say anything. She just carried on as if nothing had happened, and eventually Mrs Frost tore her eyes away from Cassie's jeans to address Greta:

'I'm terribly sorry you were kept waiting,' she smiled. 'Cassie here is a wonderful dancer, but she's not renowned for her punctuality.'

They were back in Mrs Frost's office again. This was becoming all too familiar.

'It seems to be just one thing after another,' Mrs Frost was saying. 'You show up late and dishevelled – and in jeans! – for an important visitor, you display a flagrant lack of interest in your studies, you speak carelessly to teachers. In short, you please yourself. And pleasing yourself is not what Starlight Academy is about – quite the opposite in fact. Now I have to warn you again, Cassie, you are on a knife-edge at this school.'

So it was a knife-edge this time, instead of a frozen pond. Who exactly *did* stand on a knife's edge anyway? Apart from a particularly daring dwarf. As she walked away, Mrs Frost's final words rang in her ears: 'Tread carefully,' she had said. 'Tread very carefully.'

In the dorm that night, Cassie sat ashen-faced on her bed whilst Bella explained her earlier run-in with Abigail.

'I'm really sorry, guys,' she confessed, 'but I think Abigail knows.'

'Knows?' gasped Jasmine. 'How could she know?'

'I let something slip on the coach on the way home, because I was so angry with her, and she won't let it be. She said she's been down to the woodshed, and she knows what we're up to, and she keeps on and on at me.'

'But you haven't told her have you?' said Megan. 'I mean, she might not know anything, she might be bluffing.'

'No, of course I haven't told her, but she could ruin everything if she wants to,' said Bella grimly. 'She's already threatened to tell Mrs Frost if we don't let her join in.'

'Typical!' fumed Jasmine. 'It's not enough that she's already the star of one show, she has to make herself the star of our show too. It's not fair!'

'But if we don't let her in, she'll tell Mrs Frost and then it will all be off anyway,' reasoned Bella.

'So what do we do?' asked Megan. 'Give her a part? Let her join in so that the play can still go ahead?'

All the time they were debating what was best to do, Cassie sat vacantly on her bed staring into space, a grey look of fear stretched across her face.

'What do *you* think Cassie?' asked Bella, turning to her suddenly.

Cassie was silent for a moment, and then, 'I can't do it,' she said finally. 'I just can't. It's too much of a risk. I'm sorry, but I have to pull out.'

The all protested at once, clambering over each other to get through to her, but Cassie just shook her head.

'I can't,' she insisted. 'I could be in such trouble. Mrs Frost has already warned me I'm on a knife-edge at this school. I'm so sorry, I wish I didn't have to say this, but as far as I'm concerned it's off.'

No one could quite believe what was happening. They all just stared at each other, aghast. No Woodshed Theatre. No secret performance. No gypsy caravan. It was unthinkable.

Chapter 11: *Camping Out*

Abigail caught up with Bella early on Saturday morning, as she was on her way to the Wilderness Club meeting. It was the night of the campout in the woods, and Cassie had summoned them all to the Dining Hall.

'So what have you decided?' Abigail said, 'are you going to let me in on it?'

Bella hesitated. They still hadn't decided what to do about the Abigail situation. Everything was up in the air now that Cassie had resigned.

'But ... but ... the trouble is,' she faltered, 'you're already going to be doing the school play at the same time.'

'You're going to escape during the *play*?' asked Abigail.

Bella stopped walking and turned to face Abigail.

'We're going to *what* during the play? What are you talking about *escape*?'

'Oh, don't go all innocent on me,' said Abigail, putting her hands on her hips and fixing Bella with a hard look. 'I told you, I've already seen it. I know what you're planning.'

'Seen *what* exactly?' queried Bella.

'The escape tunnel you've built. Outside that shed in

the woods. I saw it rolling around on the ground. I don't know how you're planning to do it, but I reckon you're going to put it over the moat somehow – like Cassie said in history about her bridge – and escape at night.'

Bella tried not to smile.

'So you want in on it? You want to escape with us?' she said, biting her lip.

'Yeah, of course. It'll be fun. And I can't have any fun going on without me,' she twinkled.

'OK then, sure.' Bella held up her hands in defeat. 'You can join us. Meet us outside tonight, at ten o'clock.'

'But I thought you said you were going to do it during the play,' said Abigail, frowning in confusion.

'Well, we can't if you're joining us, can we?' replied Bella. 'We'll just have to do it tonight. I'll tell the others there's been a change of plan.'

She put an arm around Abigail's shoulder. And then, thinking quickly, instructed her: 'Meet us by the willow tree – you know the one that's just out of sight of the gatehouse? That's where we're crossing the moat. With our escape tunnel.'

Despite her run-ins with Cassie, Mrs Frost had stood by her promise to let the Wilderness Club spend a night camping out in the woods. But no one was in the mood for it any more except for Cassie. None of the others cared whether it went ahead or not, because what difference did it make anyway if the play was off? The whole point of the weekend camp-out had been to rehearse the play, build the caravan and finish the scenery. Now, none of that would be happening and everything was pointless. Only Cassie remained enthusiastic: since abandoning the play, she had decided to throw herself into Wilderness Club with even more gusto and was taking it all very seriously.

She had assembled the Wilderness Club girls in the dining hall after breakfast on Saturday morning and was delivering strict instructions: 'Right, you've got half an hour to get all your stuff together. Just the bare minimum. We'll meet back here at ten o'clock precisely. Mr Swann is going to help us get our camp set up and then leave us to it.'

The girls set off reluctantly, but Cassie called them back immediately and carried on in her strict, bossy voice, 'Just so you know, no mobiles, no iPods, no make-up, no jewellery. If you bring them, they'll be confiscated.'

'Yes Miss March, no Miss March, whatever you say Miss March,' muttered Bella.

Megan and Flo had only joined Wilderness Club so that they could rehearse the play, so now they were less keen than ever about the prospect of camping out in the woods.

'Oh, let me at least bring my mattress and duvet out,' pleaded Flo mournfully. 'I don't see why we have to sleep on the ground. I mean what were beds invented for if not for us to sleep on?'

'Look, you're missing the point,' said Cassie, wearily. 'We're meant to be relying on nature. You know, getting away from all the comforts of modern life and seeing how much we can do without.'

'I'll be so glad when I'm safely back in my warm bed tomorrow night,' said Megan as they went up to the dorms to sort themselves out.

'Oh, have a teensy sense of adventure will you!' groaned an exasperated Cassie.

'"We'll have too much work to do building our shelters and foraging for food,' said Cassie sternly, 'never mind looking up at the stars.'

In the woods, it was cold and windy. The girls stood in a huddle, hugging themselves against the stiff breeze. Only Cassie seemed enthralled as Mr Swann taught them how to set up sleeping shelters. He had already cut down a pile of long, strong sticks and he showed them how to lash them together with bendy tree roots to form a sloping roof.

'Actually the best natural string is made from animal muscles or intestines,' he explained.

'Yuk, revolting!' said Flo. 'Hmm, let's see,' she shivered, 'sleep inside in your normal bed or make a house out of some poor animal's stomach so that you can sleep out in the cold? How am I ever going to choose?'

'Outside any day for me,' said Cassie, 'you can always sleep in a boring old bed.'

'I think my violin strings are made of catgut,' said Megan, shivering and pulling up her hood, 'but that's at least in a good cause.'

'Oh, that's why it wails so much,' joked Flo, 'poor cat!'

'Actually,' said Mr Swann, 'the old way of stringing instruments never used the guts of cats, but more often goat or sheep guts. The expression "catgut" is thought to derive from a shortening of "cattle gut".'

'Mr Swann, you're so nerdy, it's brilliant,' said Bella. 'You know so much detail about so many pointless things, it's fab.'

Mr Swann frowned, unsure as to whether he was being insulted or not.

Next, he taught them how to thatch their shelters with moss and bracken to keep the rain off. They joined in dutifully, poking bunches of leaves between the joins.

'Always start from the bottom upwards,' said Mr Swann, 'that way, the rain will roll over the joins and won't drip inside the shelter.'

'Wait a second,' said Flo, 'you're not seriously telling me that we're actually sleeping under one of these things tonight. I mean I can see it's clever and everything, but not for real.'

Mr Swann laughed, 'Well, I thought you might feel that way, so I've brought along an old army-style canvas tent from my scouting days, one that will fit you all. You can help me put it up before I go.'

Cassie was distraught, 'Oh please, I beg you, let me sleep in this shelter. It's hardly a real wilderness experience if we sleep in a tent from a shop.'

Mr Swann shrugged, 'What you get up to when I've gone is strictly your own business. Assuming of course that you're going to be safe and sensible. This sort of shelter will protect you from the worst of the weather and help to prevent the loss of heat from your body during the night, but if it rains I would suggest you go in the tent with everyone else.'

Cassie was so excited to be camping properly in the wild that she could hardly contain herself.

'And tell them the bit about using your senses fully for survival and peripheral vision and all that,' she urged Mr Swann.

'Well, that is mainly for areas of genuine danger. These woods are of course enclosed within the school grounds, and I can safely assure you that there are no wild animals about,' he laughed.

'I know, I know, but say there were,' said Cassie, taking over and addressing the uninterested audience, 'what you do is sit incredibly still, opening up your senses and letting them travel out as far as you can. It's amazing what you can hear and smell. And you can even kind of see behind you – well, in a way.'

'Come on, let's cook those chocolate orange things,' said Bella, 'I'm starving.'

Cassie tried to hide her disappointment that no one was taking it as seriously as her.

'Strictly speaking those chocolate orange things are cheating,' she said, disapprovingly.

'Oh who cares, I think it's a great idea of Jasmine's. Tell us again, Jas.'

'Well, you cut the top off the orange and scoop out the insides and eat them, then you fill the hole with chocolate cake mix – I've got a packet here and you just mix it with water – then put them in the fire for ten minutes and – ta da! – you have your chocolate orange cake. Simply break open the orange to find your cake.'

'Most useful tip I've learnt all day,' said Bella.

Cassie tried to get their attention back to survival skills, 'Tell them about all the leaves you can eat, Mr Swann.'

Mr Swann took a bunch of assorted leaves from one of his many inner pockets.

'Well, there are dandelion leaves of course,' he said, munching one with relish, 'delicious! The best food in the world – what nature leaves on our doorstep. Surprisingly, you can also eat nettles, and then there's sorrel, burdock …'

But Bella broke in, 'Look you two nature geeks can eat all the stinging nettles you like if that's what you really fancy. I'm going to stick to these chocolate oranges, thanks very much.'

*   *   *

As soon as Mr Swann had left, everyone apart from Cassie jumped up and went off to get the paint and brushes stored inside the woodshed. They hauled the caravan frame out of the shed and set it down right in front of Cassie, then they got to work, laughing and chatting as they painted fat bright flowers all over the tightly-stretched canvas.

'What are you doing?' asked Cassie. 'It's over.'

'Not for us it isn't,' said Bella gleefully. 'We're going ahead whether *you* like it or not. It's *As We Like It* remember?'

Cassie stomped off in a huff to find some dandelion leaves, and Bella gave the others a wink.

'She won't last long,' she declared.

When Jasmine found Cassie, she was furiously tearing up dandelion leaves and throwing them into a pot of water.

'Do you want a hand?' she asked.

Cassie shrugged, 'Don't want to drag you away from your precious play,' she muttered sulkily.

There was no reply, and when Cassie looked around she saw that Jasmine was crying.

'I wouldn't admit it to anyone else,' she sniffed, 'but I'm so proud of what I've written, and it we don't do the play, no one will ever hear it.'

Cassie stared at Jasmine, her face creased with anxiety.

'But you can all still go ahead and do it yourselves, Bella said so.'

Jasmine shook her head, 'No we can't. Not without you. You started the whole thing up, and you've organised it all. We might pretend we can, but we can't really. You know that.'

Her shoulders dropped and she drew a grubby sleeve across her nose.

'OK then,' Cassie grinned, 'I give in.'

She stood up and held her hand out to Jasmine.

'Come on, I've got a dance to teach you lot.'

They all cheered when Cassie joined them again, and after that they worked happily for two hours, some painting the background scenery, others laying down the planks for the stage in front of the woodshed, some going up the ladder to fix the long curtain rope between two trees, and others stringing up the circle of tea-lights which Tom and Milo would light on the night. They wouldn't actually hang the curtain until the day of the performance, but already it was beginning to look like a proper theatre. The girls who were in Wilderness Club but had nothing to do with the secret play were keen to be involved and happily acted as prompts and prop-mistresses.

By six o'clock that evening, they were sitting around a camp-fire, cooking sausages on toasting forks and telling scary stories. It was still light, but the sky was scuffed and smoky, and their faces were pinked by the setting sun as they sat and listened to the end of Jasmine's story.

'*So she locked the door and threw the key down the well in the garden and never revealed to anyone what was behind the door. But every night, when the finger tapped three times on her bedroom window, she tapped back to say "I promise I will".*'

Jasmine finished her story and they all shuddered in the silence.

'I wonder how Abigail's getting on over by the moat,' said Bella, her eyes sparkling with mischief.

'I can't believe she fell for that,' laughed Cassie.

'Poor Abi,' said Flo. 'What will she do when she realises we're not there?'

'Well, I left a special surprise for her – under the willow tree – a shoe-box full of frogs. I fished them out of the moat. She'll shriek when she sees them and the security guard in the gatehouse will come over. Ha ha! Serves her right.'

'Trouble is, she might tell Mrs Frost now,' said Megan with an anxious frown.

'Tell her what?' shrugged Bella. 'She doesn't actually know anything about the play.'

'Come on you lot,' said Cassie, standing up and brushing the twigs and leaves off her clothes. 'We've got about an hour of light left. Let's go through the dance routine again and then do a complete run-through on the stage.'

In the middle of the night, when Megan had finally stopped reading and turned down the lamp, and Flo and Bella had finally finished rolling into each other to get more sleeping room, and everyone had finally begun to drift off, Jasmine suddenly sat up.

'I've just had an idea about the play,' she whispered loudly.

'What now?' Flo muttered irritably.

'At the end, they put on a show for the other orphans they left behind, and the orphans all get to join the circus too and they all roll away in the gypsy caravan.'

'OK then,' said Flo dozily, and they all promptly fell back to sleep.

The next morning, stiff and tired from turning all night on the hard, prickly ground, they crawled out of the tent to find Cassie kicking hopefully at the dying embers of the fire.

'It's no good,' she said, 'it's completely gone out. But I had the *best* night's sleep!' she stretched and yawned contentedly.

Somehow, even though they copied exactly the methods Mr Swann had taught them and feathered a twig into curling ribbons to light the fire, they couldn't get the fire going again and soon they were all cold and hungry and fed up.

'What now?' asked Flo gloomily.

'The woodshed, of course,' chirped Cassie cheerily. She was the only one who thought that the worse things got, the better it all was. They made hot chocolate on the stove in the woodshed and shared around the few tin mugs between them. Then Bella delighted them all by producing three packs of chocolate chip cookies from her rucksack.

'I know it's strictly against the "find our food from what's around us in nature" thing, but who knows? Maybe there was a chocolate chip cookie tree growing somewhere around here once. We'll never know.'

Cassie glared at her sternly and Bella held out the packet.

'You're welcome to eat leaves instead if you like, but here they are if you want one.'

They all tucked in eagerly, even Cassie, who finally admitted that she didn't really like dandelion leaves.

When they had warmed up and were feeling more cheerful, they decided to have a final run-through before packing up their camp and going back to school for Sunday lunch. They tried out the last scene with Jasmine's new addition of the performance at the orphanage. Many of the lines were improvised as they went along, but Jasmine had given them a good idea of how it should go. Her grand finale involved all the orphans – who were now to be played by the rest of the girls in Wilderness Club – jumping onto the back of the gypsy caravan as the circus-master-turned-long-lost-father cracked his whip and called out to the strict orphanage mistress: '*We're taking these poor girls with us to join our circus.*'

And the outraged orphanage mistress responding, '*But you can't! I won't have it!*'

And then Bella had the final line when she shouted back, '*From now on Miss Pinchface, it's not going to be as* you *like it, but as* we *like it.*'

And that was the cue for clapping. Cassie and Flo took the place of Tom and Milo and tried to pull the caravan offstage, but they couldn't even lift it, let alone shift it, so everyone had to jump off and help push. By the end, they had all collapsed on the floor in a heap of laughter.

'There's only one last thing,' said Cassie whilst they tidied all the props away into the woodshed. 'What are you going to say to announce the play, Jasmine?'

Jasmine dropped what she was doing and turned, horror-struck, to face Cassie.

'What do you mean what am I going to say?'

'Well, you wrote the play, and someone has to introduce it, and the rest of us are acting in it, so it's obvious you should come on stage first and make an announcement about how it all happened.'

'But I can't,' Jasmine stammered.

'Jasmine!' said Flo, 'You've been on stage loads of times before – you're a dancer!'

'But that's completely different!' Jasmine's voice

was weakly pleading. 'I can't just stand up there as me, Jasmine, and talk. I'd die of embarrassment.'

It was lunch time by then, and they were all in high spirits but also starving, so it didn't take them long to dismantle their camp, scatter the cold embers of the fire and lock up the door of the Woodshed Theatre.

'We won't open it again until the day of the performance,' said Bella with a conspiratorial grin. 'I can't wait.'

Chapter 12: *Double Drama*

The morning of the school production of *As You Like It* was the same as it always was on production day – everyone ran about in a hyperactive frenzy and the air crackled with excitement. Abigail and Lauren came into breakfast looking like the joint ruling queens of the school, and everybody seemed to be fussing over them. If they'd been royal brides they would have been straightening their trains, but as it was they settled for fanning them with scripts.

'Oh my god, I'm so stressed,' Abigail kept saying, running a suitably stressed hand through her sideways fringe.

The Fonteyn girls were also feeling stressed, but theirs was a secret stress, which they couldn't keep blurting out. They contented themselves instead with giving each other knowing looks and going over the play privately in their heads, as a sort of mental dress-rehearsal. They all found it difficult to get their breakfast past the knot of excitement in their stomachs, and there was a lot of pushing cereal around bowls with spoons.

The performance of *As You Like It* was due to start at three pm and by two o'clock parents had started to arrive for an afternoon tea of scones and jam, which was served on the front lawn. None of the Fonteyn girls were directly involved in the official play since Megan and Flo had pulled out of the music, but at the last minute Cassie had volunteered to help out moving scenery onstage. She needed all the brownie points she could get. At three o'clock, Miss Spitzer sat cast and crew down together in the assembly hall and played them a CD which told them in an annoying voice how great and powerful they were and how the light of the universe shone through them. Then she took them through a guided meditation which involved lying on the floor and feeling the creative force of the universe flow through every inch of their bodies. This sort of thing would have been fine if Miss Flanders had done it with them: they would have entered into the spirit of it. But Miss Spitzer was using one of those falsely calm voices, which underneath isn't calm at all, and she really did list every tiny particle of their bodies in an infuriatingly slow voice. And while she purred quietly, '*Feel that powerful force rushing into every single molecule of every single hair on your head, feel it wakening up the muscles around your eyes, let it flow into your eyelashes, each – and – every – one – of – them*', they could sense that really she was thinking in a hard, fraught voice, '*Please don't let them mess this up and make me look a fool!*'

Throughout the meditation, all anyone could think about was what they wanted to be doing instead – either having one last look at their lines, or going over the lighting sequence, or having a last rifle through the costumes on the rail to check the labelling. But instead, they had to lie on the floor of the assembly hall until it was nearly time for the performance. As a result, there was a last minute panic during which Abigail shrieked, 'Where's my dress for the first scene? It's gone. There's been a mix-up. I can't wear this jester's outfit.'

The costume was discovered, but the effect of Abigail's shrieking was like a stone being thrown into a pond full of ducks, and as the music struck up for the opening scene, there was mayhem behind stage.

*   *   *

As Cassie was tiptoeing offstage in the darkness before the final scene of the first half, a mischievous thought suddenly struck her. She had just put a fake log in place, which Abigail as Rosalind would sit on periodically during the forest scenes, and she had been thinking how stupid it looked, how unlike a real log in a real forest, when the thought crept up on her. Without taking the time to decide if it was a good idea or not, she rushed for the back door as soon as the first half was over and dashed off towards the woods. It didn't take her long to find what she was looking for – on the very first tree she came to there was a wedge of loose bark with hundreds of tiny creatures scuttling around behind it. She prised the bark off the tree carefully and slipped it into a plastic bag that she had taken from the costume room, then ran back to the theatre to help prepare the stage for the second half before the end of the interval.

Sitting in the audience, Bella had to admit to herself that Abigail was a fabulous actress. She may only have been in Year 7, but she acted with the maturity and conviction of a proper grown woman. Bella even had the honesty to admit that she made a better job of Rosalind than she would have done herself. She was wise and passionate, but also funny and reckless when she had to be. It wasn't an easy thing to admit and she felt a sharp claw of jealousy digging away at her throughout the whole first half, so she couldn't help feeling cheered by the incident that set off the second half. Rosalind had just sat down on the fake log to read the poem she found stuck to a tree, but before she had got very far, she let out a high-pitched squeal and leapt up off the log. Throwing the poem aside, she ran around the stage in circles, shaking her legs and arms and trying to brush something off her.

'Get it off!' she kept hissing at Lauren as Celia, who only looked at her in adoring wonder. Then Lauren noticed the hunk of bark on the fake log and saw the woodlice and earwigs crawling all over it and guessed what the problem was, so she escorted Abigail to the other side of the stage. The audience meanwhile, weren't sure whether this was part of the play or not. Some of them laughed at the clever joke of a city girl coming into contact with real country life in the forest. Some just laughed at the sight of Abigail flailing about on stage. And others exchanged baffled looks. Mrs Frost looked at Miss Spitzer with raised eyebrows for an explanation, while Miss Spitzer just stared in horror and fury at Abigail. It was all over in a minute, and Bella had to admit (yet again) that Abigail handled it like a pro. Once she had got rid of the offending creepy-crawlies, she picked up the poem from the floor, crossed to the other side of the stage as far away from the fake log as possible, and ad-libbed an extra line 'Methinks some vile creatures have crept into my clothes' with a smile at the audience. Then the play carried on and it was generally considered to have been a great success.

Straight after the performance, a crowd of girls gathered around Miss Flanders, who had returned from Scotland to see the play. She had slipped in late at the back because her train had been delayed. The girls were so pleased to see her that they huddled around her and all talked at once in their eagerness to find out when she would be back. She looked thinner than when she had left, and somehow older, with grey bags under her eyes and colourless cheeks.

'Why did she send you away?' whispered Bella urgently, 'was it because of that stunt in the woods? Because if it was, I'm so, so sorry and I swear, since then I've given up playing tricks on people – well, almost ...'

'Hush, hush, hush,' giggled Miss Flanders, some colour returning to her cheeks instantly, 'No of course it wasn't that, you silly girl! Mrs Frost didn't send me away. I had to go and look after my step-mother, who is dying.'

There was an awful hush.

'Oh, then I'm even more sorry,' said Bella. 'You must be very upset.'

Miss Flanders laughed weakly, 'Well, actually she's a cantankerous old woman who has been awful to me all my life. But I'm all she's got.'

'She's awful to you even now? When you're looking after her so kindly?'

'Oh yes, worse than ever. Calls me all sorts of dreadful names. But, like I said, I'm all she's got, and you can't just abandon people because they're bad tempered. Occasionally, just occasionally, she smiles at me and says thank you, and that makes it all bearable again.'

'But when will you be back?'

'I don't know. Soon perhaps. We'll have to wait and see.'

It was only then that they suddenly remembered.

'Oh, Miss Flanders!' yelped Bella, 'Just wait! Just wait and see what a treat we've got in store for you!'

'You are coming to the Wilderness Club demonstration after supper aren't you?' said Jasmine nervously.

'Well, I suppose so, as I'm here,' she laughed.

'Mr Swann will be pleased to see you,' said Bella with a grin, and Miss Flanders responded by whacking her on the head with her play programme.

Jasmine was leading her parents and Grandparents down to the woods for the Wilderness Club demonstration. It was beginning to get dark, just the perfect light for their play. Jasmine's parents were telling her how impressed they had been by Abigail's performance, and she was trying to listen and trying to respond, but her heart was racing and her stomach was churning so much that she could hardly hear them. She couldn't get out of her mind what Cassie had said about introducing the play. She really, really didn't want to. But then how would the play start? It couldn't just roll slowly into action like an old horse and cart. Something would have to kick-start it. Perhaps one of the others would do it. But who? She knew there was no real plan about how it would all get under way. They had only talked about how they would get everyone down to the woods, and how when they got there they would see the theatre, and the rows of log benches, with the curtains drawn across the stage, and the string of lights glowing in a high circle around the stage. They hoped against hope that Mrs Frost would be too bewitched by the charming sight of it all to be angry, and they knew of course that she couldn't just explode in front of the parents. She would have to at least go along with it while the parents were there. Beyond that, they hadn't really planned. The play itself would only last for about half an hour, including the acrobatic display from Milo, and Cassie's dance.

'Oh, that's Abigail Rowan there, is it?'

Her gran's voice broke in on her thoughts and she looked up.

'Yes, that's her,' said Jasmine absent-mindedly.

'Well, she certainly deserves that scholarship. She's got a real talent there.'

Abigail was just about to pass them when Jasmine's gran called out, 'Abigail!'

Abigail came over, looking a little surprised.

'Hello, dear. I just wanted to congratulate you on a fine performance. Actually, I know your father well. He does my garden. I must say, I couldn't do without him.'

Abigail just stared hard at Jasmine's gran and didn't say anything, although her face turned a kind of ashy white.

'What do you mean he does your garden?' asked Jasmine. 'You mean he does gardening too, when he's not directing.'

'Oh, I don't know about directing, but he's certainly a wonderful gardener.'

By then they had reached the site of the Woodshed Theatre and there were gasps of delight from all the parents. It did look magical, with the tiny lights twinkling through the darkness and shadows flickering across the heavy red velvet curtain strung between the trees. The stage was edged with large grey pebbles and sea-shells, which they had collected from the beach, and Cassie had painted a sign on the left-over velvet saying: 'Welcome to the Woodshed Theatre production of *As We Like It.*'

She should have felt so proud, but somehow Jasmine couldn't enjoy it at all. She was too scared. She just wished it would all be over. Cassie walked up and put an arm around her shoulder.

'Ready, Jasmine?' she said.

And Jasmine knew what she had to do. It was like splashing cold water on your face in the morning: your hands never wanted to do it, but you had to just make them.

All the parents were sitting down on the log benches, and the rest of Years 7 and 8 were sitting cross-legged on the rugs at the front. Jasmine stood on her own in the middle of the stage and took a deep breath. Her knees were literally knocking against each other – she hadn't known they could really do that – and she felt that she might at any moment just fall over. Her heart thundered in her throat and her mouth felt dry, in fact, it felt as if her tongue might never unstick from the top of her mouth. She tried to encourage herself by thinking of all the times she had danced on a stage, but it made no difference. When she danced she was a different person, not this shy, blushing, nervous Jasmine. She hadn't planned what she would say, but she knew suddenly that it would have to be a poem and she would have to make it up on the spot. She began with the first line, speaking slowly and carefully and making sure everyone had time to hear each word: 'We're glad that you've come to our woodland show …'

After that first line, the words just seemed to flow out of her mouth. She had no idea where they came from, but she didn't stop to think about it. She just stood there and recited her poem:

'We're glad that you've come to our woodland show
And we hope you'll have some fun before you go.
We wrote it ourselves, so please be forgiving, I'm not
Shakespeare – I don't do this for a living.
But Daisy did the music and Cassie did the dances
We rehearsed it in secret – we took our chances.
We tidied up the woodshed and gave it a lick of paint
We worked so hard we thought we would faint.

*Mrs Frost always says we should reach for the stars
And that's what we've done with this play of ours.'*

The parents laughed and clapped all the way through the performance of *As We Like It*. It was a mish-mash of different styles and pieces, and many of the lines were haltingly made up as they went along, but it was all so joyous and so impulsive. It seemed to sum up everything that Spring was about. At the end of the play, as Tom and Milo jogged off into the woods, pulling the creaky caravan full of girls behind them with great difficulty, everyone stood up and cheered. And then, when it was all over, so many parents remarked to Mrs Frost how wonderful it was that she encouraged such initiative in her pupils, all she could do was smile.

After the play, they were due to go home for a long weekend. It was past eight o'clock and everyone was tired after the day's double drama, but Mr Swann had insisted that they return the pebbles and seashells back to the beach where they belonged, and Cassie couldn't resist the chance to go down to the sea-shore.

'I'll come with you,' Flo volunteered.

'You go too, Tom, to keep an eye on her,' Flo's mum added quickly. 'I don't want her falling headlong down a cliff at this time of night.'

'It would be OK for her to fall headlong down a cliff in the morning I suppose,' muttered Tom.

'Oh, let's all just go,' said Jasmine.

So they all helped Mr Swann and Miss Flanders return

the pebbles and shells back to the beach, while their parents packed up the cars.

As they walked along, Jasmine explained the odd exchange between her gran and Abigail.

'It's a bit of a mystery,' she said, 'because if he's a gardener how does he have time to be a film director too? And if he's a film director, why would he want to be a gardener as well?'

'It's not all that much of a mystery if you ask me,' said Cassie. 'He's probably not a film director at all. I mean, we've only got her word for it and she's not exactly the most trustworthy person I've ever met.'

'But what about the premiere and all that?' said Tom. 'I mean, we definitely went to it, and the people that escorted us knew her name and we were picked up by a limo and everything. Her dad's got to be *something* to do with it.'

They thought about it for a while but no one could come up with a reasonable explanation.

'Well, whatever the truth is,' said Jasmine, 'I think we should make up with Abigail. She's not all that bad really. In fact, she can be really friendly.'

'Yeah, it's just that she doesn't like to be friendly to the same person for too long,' added Bella.

'Well, if she has to make up stuff about herself just to impress people, she must feel really bad about herself. It must be horrible to think that your family aren't good enough so you have to make up a new family.'

Mr Swann and Miss Flanders were walking ahead of them talking, and occasionally as they walked their shoulders would bump into each other. Bella elbowed Jasmine and whispered, 'Sssh! Look. I *knew* it.'

'Stop right there, Bella,' said Megan. 'No more clever schemes.'

'Hey!' whined Bella, 'that's not fair. I haven't done anything for ages.'

Down on the beach, Cassie kicked off her shoes, ran towards the quietly ebbing sea and was paddling before Miss Flanders had time to protest.

'Eek!' she yelled, 'it's f-f-f-f FREEZING! Come on you lot, come in. The water's lovely and warm,' she shivered.

No one would, except for Tom, who couldn't turn down a challenge from a girl. As they hopped from one foot to another, trying to get some feeling back into their feet, he bent down and picked up a medium-sized crab.

'Here. Present for you,' he said, handing it to Cassie. 'It's like when they throw flowers onto the stage for the dancer at the end of a performance. Except it's a crab.'

Cassie examined the crab in delight.

'I love it! Much better than flowers. In fact, I'm going to keep it as a pet. I'll bring it back to school in a tank after the weekend, and I'll call it … Nipper.'

'Or how about Pincham?'

'OK, Pincham.'

* * *

There was one final event before the end of term: a visit

152

to the children's hospital that Tara was raising money for. Tara had organised for Years 7 and 8 to have a tour of the hospital, ending up at the outside space which was going to be cleared in preparation for the Starlight Garden. They stood and looked at the large patch of weedy scrubland and Tara sighed.

'It would have been so amazing for them. It was going to have a maze and a tree-house and everything.'

'What do you mean?' asked Cassie. 'Why "would have"? Isn't it going to happen? I thought you raised the money.'

'Well, I haven't raised nearly as much as I thought I would, and the person who was going to landscape the garden for free had to pull out, so it looks like the children won't have their Starlight Garden after all.'

Cassie thought for a moment.

'Hey look, my dad designs tree-houses,' she said. 'He could do something really cool for this garden, I know he could. And I know he'd do it for free. But he can't do gardens. He'd be rubbish at that. He can't even cut the grass without mowing off his own feet.' She paused for a moment, giving it time to sink in. 'So what we really need is a gardener. A really good gardener. Someone who would do it for free. But I guess that's not very likely.'

Before she could stop herself, Abigail had said, 'I bet my dad would do it.'

'Oh, is he a gardener as well as a director?' asked Tara.

'Well actually, he's just a gardener, not a director,' said Abigail quietly.

There was an awkward silence. Then Cassie said,

'Well, that's great. You might have just solved our problem. Do you really think he would do it?'

'Yeah, I'm sure he would,' said Abigail with a smile.

'So how come?' asked Bella, as they walked back to the coach. 'How come all the stuff about him being a director on *Wild Thing*. And all the other film stuff.'

'I suppose it all started when I won tickets to the premiere,' Abigail explained. 'I entered a competition in a magazine and I won. I couldn't believe it – limo service, after-show party and everything. Two tickets. I suppose that gave me the idea. You see, I'm here on a scholarship, but I'm desperate not to be a scholarship girl. I don't want everyone feeling sorry for me for being poor. And when I started hearing about what all your parents did, I couldn't bear to say that my dad was a gardener.'

Bella put a friendly arm around her shoulder, 'I'll swap you a gardener for a yoghurt-maker.'

'So, how come you have so much money to spend on clothes?' asked Jasmine, looking enviously at Abigail's latest pair of trainers.

'I don't really. My poor dad. He works so hard already and there I am demanding more and more money. I told him if he sends me to a school like Starlight Academy he's got to pay to get me the kind of clothes they wear here.'

'But we don't all wear designer clothes at all!' protested Jasmine. 'I mean, look at me, and look at Flo, for goodness' sake!'

'Thanks!' laughed Flo.

'Well, I know that now,' said Abigail, 'but at first before I came here I thought you'd all be really top labels and everything, so I bought all this stuff. And then I kind of got hooked on it, and nothing else seemed good enough.'

They sat on the back row of the coach with Abigail and Lauren, the synthetic twins reunited, and talked all the way back to school. Lauren was the only one who had known Abigail's secret all along, and the only one, it turned out, who had been a true friend to her by keeping it.

By the time Miss Flanders came back the next term, everyone had forgotten about the Abigail situation, and when Mrs Frost talked about the fantastic production of *As You Like It*, she sometimes called it *As We Like It* by mistake, but that was the only time she ever mentioned it. Cassie redeemed herself in Mrs Frost's eyes by donating her gypsy caravan to the Starlight Garden and by setting up a drama club at the Woodshed Theatre for children from the Riverside Hospital. Miss Spitzer ran the club with earnest attention to detail – once she had scrubbed and disinfected the hut, of course – and despite her motivational talks encouraging them to be unicorns and butterflies, it seemed that the children really did manage to have a 'whole bunch of fun'. So in the end, it all turned out pretty much as everyone liked it.

Look out for Book 1 in the Starlight Academy series

STARLIGHT ACADEMY

Welcome to Starlight Academy the fairytale castle by the sea where dreams come true for girls with a passion for performing!

Cassie March is a free-spirited dancer, who feels stifled by the endless rules and restrictions of school life. Cassie's used to doing her own thing, so it's no surprise that she ends up in regular battles with Starlight's strict headmistress, Mrs Frost.

As the school production of the Nutcracker approaches, Cassie finds herself pitched against Tara Davenport, the school's best dancer. She's determined to land the lead role, and she could be in with a chance – if she could only stay out of trouble. Will her best friend – law abiding but scatty Flo – manage to keep her in line? And will her secret dream ever come true?